Also by Kellie Hailes

The Cosy Coffee Shop of Promises

At the age of five, **Kellie Hailes** declared she was going to write books when she grew up. It took a while for her to get there, with a career as a radio copywriter, freelance copywriter and web writer filling the dream-hole, until now. Kellie lives on an island-that's-not-really-an-island in New Zealand with her patient husband, funny little human and neurotic cat. When the characters in her head aren't dictating their story to her, she can be found taking short walks, eating good cheese and jonesing for her next coffee fix.

The Big Little Festival

Kellie Hailes

ONE PLACE. MANY STORIES

HarperCollins PUBLISHERS
— Since 1817 —

This novel is entirely a work of fiction. The names, characters and incidents portrayed in it are the work of the author's imagination. Any resemblance to actual persons, living or dead, events or localities is entirely coincidental.

HQ
An imprint of HarperCollins*Publishers* Ltd
1 London Bridge Street
London SE1 9GF

This paperback edition 2017

1

First published in Great Britain by
HQ, an imprint of HarperCollins*Publishers* Ltd 2017

Copyright © Kellie Hailes 2017

Kellie Hailes asserts the moral right to be identified as the author of this work.
A catalogue record for this book is available from the British Library.

ISBN: 978-0-00-827446-7

MIX
Paper from
responsible sources
FSC™ C007454

This book is produced from independently certified FSC™ paper to ensure responsible forest management.

For more information visit: www.harpercollins.co.uk/green

Printed and bound in Great Britain by
CPI Group, Croydon CR0 4YY

For Daisy,
I love you to the ends of the ever-expanding universe.

CHAPTER ONE

Let's have a festival, they said. *It'll be great for the town*, they said. *You're head of the PTA, you'll make a great festival committee head*, they said.

Finally, she'd thought, relief easing the ever-present guilt that years ago had settled in the back of her mind, and deep in her heart. *The chance I've been waiting for to right my wrongs.*

Jody sank back into the village hall's burnt-orange-coloured plastic chair and resisted the urge to bang her forehead repeatedly on the dirty, cream-coloured foldaway table before her. She'd known taking on the festival was going to be a big job, but she'd had no idea just how big. The admin alone was mind-boggling, but it was a walk in the park compared to dealing with the two women sitting before her.

'People. Won't. Come. If. We. Don't. Have. Clowns.' With every word, Shirley Harper banged the table with the flat of her palm, as if hoping she might knock some sense into her fellow festival committee members.

'People. Won't. Come. If. We. *Do*. Have. Clowns.' Marjorie Hunter jabbed the air in Shirley's direction, punctuating her point. 'Clowns. Scare. People.'

Jody rubbed her temples, hoping to ease the throb that appeared every time they held a meeting. 'What if we had one clown? A friendly looking one. They could juggle, make balloon animals. Do magic tricks?' She put the idea out there and prayed it would stick.

'One clown makes us look cheap.' Mrs Harper folded her arms across her bosomy chest. 'And we don't do cheap in Rabbits Leap.'

Jody stifled a snort. Rabbits Leap didn't do cheap? Since when? The town had been living on a shoestring for as long as she could remember. That was until her brother, Tony, and his fiancée, Mel, had breathed life into the old pub and attracted the attention of outsiders. Their success had seen the whole town wanting a bit of the action, and they'd decided the five-hundredth anniversary of the Rabbit Revolt was the perfect opportunity to bring people into the village – in the form of a festival. A way to bring money into businesses while fundraising to revive the community pool.

'Are you sure we don't do cheap, Shirley?' Mrs Hunter's eyes widened. An innocent look that belied the snide tone of her words. 'Because those court shoes of yours hardly look like they've come from some fancy high-end store. Or maybe they did and I didn't realise scuffed vinyl was in fashion...'

Mrs Harper's chest puffed out in outrage. 'I always thought you were a bit of a hoity-toity co—'

'Ladies, ladies...' Jody raised her hands in the hope of bringing the sniping to a halt. 'Let's not let something that's meant to be fun become the opposite. We're all friends, remember? And if we're not friends, we're still neighbours and we still have to—'

'You two. Get off there. At once.'

The authoritative voice rumbled through the hall's open doors, stopping Jody's attempt at peacemaking in its tracks. She knew immediately who the directive was aimed at.

Oh God, what had the boys done now?

Jody scraped the chair back. The ugly screech of metal legs on wood had the unexpected effect of stopping Mrs Harper and Mrs Hunter from staring at each other mutinously, instead making them turn their attention to her.

'I've got to go check on the boys. I'll be back. Play nice,' she ordered as she stalked out of the gloomy hall into the bright summer sun and hurried across the road to the park where she'd left the boys to play during the meeting.

'If you two don't get off there right now I shall come over and take you down myself.'

Jody broke into a trot. There was no way she was letting anyone touch her boys, whether they were misbehaving or not.

'What's going on over there?' she called out, slowing down as she approached the back of Tyler and Jordan's accuser – tall, broad shouldered and far too well dressed, in a crisp white polo shirt and khaki-coloured tailored cargo shorts, to be a local.

'These two are climbing all over that sculpture. What if they damage it? Where are their parents? And shouldn't they be in school?'

Jody stifled a snort as she looked at the 'artwork'. The boys were hardly going to damage it considering it was made from stainless steel and built to withstand at least ten times their weight. When the parish council had decided to turn an empty lot into a communal area for people to relax or have picnics, she'd offered to donate an artwork that not only represented Rabbits Leap but also doubled as a piece of playground equipment. Why slide on a slide when you could slip down the back of a big steel rabbit in mid leap?

'Do you know who they are? Can you get them off?'

The stranger turned to face Jody. His coffee-coloured eyes blazed with intensity, wiping the amused grin off her face. Who was this man, with those eyes that could pin a woman to a wall, lush lips that looked entirely too kissable, and… And why was she thinking about him like this? She didn't do that. She'd trained herself to see men as women with an extra appendage. They weren't sexy. She didn't want to kiss them. And pinning her to the wall was out of the question.

Jody swallowed, hoping the act would return moisture to her parched throat. Return sanity. No such luck.

She forced herself to look away from the man, who was unknowingly questioning her parenting ability, and turned her attention to the boys.

'Boys! You get your little backsides off there, right this instant.' She watched the stranger's reaction out of the corner of her eye as her mum-tone caught Jordan and Tyler's attention.

'Do we have to?' Jordan pouted.

'The slide's the best thing about this park.' Tyler made no effort to get down, and instead clambered up towards the top of the rabbit and sat between its ears.

She raised an eyebrow. 'Don't make me tell you twice.'

'Oh, so these are your charges? You're their nanny?'

Jody mashed her lips together and forced the laugh down. Nanny? Who had nannies in Rabbits Leap? Seriously, what world did this guy come from?

'I'm their something,' she replied, trying to keep a straight face.

One thump. Another. Followed by the soft patter of bare feet on lush green grass.

'Mum.' Jordan folded his skinny arms across his thin chest in disapproval. 'You suck. That rabbit's the *only* thing to play on.'

'Yeah, you suck.' Tyler echoed his older-by-four-minutes brother and drove the heel of his foot into the lawn, putting a dent in the turf. 'There's nothing else to do. We tried lying on the grass and making up cloud animals, but it got booooooring. Besides, it's not a "sculpture", it's a slide. We're allowed to play on it.'

'You're their mother?' The handsome interloper turned towards Jody, his head angled in surprise. 'You hardly look old enough. And are you going to just let that one tear up the grass?'

Jody drew in a breath in an attempt to keep her cool. 'I'm well old enough, thank you very much.' She raised a warning eyebrow at Tyler, who stilled his feet with an unimpressed glare.

'You see, with the festival nearly here, everything must look perfect...' The stranger stopped, and then took a step back. 'Which is why I'm here, and I'm looking for someone. I don't suppose you know Jody McArthur and where I could find her?'

Jody wavered between telling a lie and sending the man on his way, or telling the truth and having him save her bacon. An outraged squawk floated on the warm breeze from the direction of the hall. Damn it. She'd have to tell the truth.

'Christian Middlemore, I presume?'

His eyes flared in surprise. 'And you've come to this conclusion how?'

'You're the man who's going to sort out this crazy festival mess we've got ourselves into. And I'm Jody McArthur, sculptor of that damn rabbit, and head of the festival committee.' She thrust her hand forward. 'I'm relieved to meet you.'

Christian's lips parted in shock. 'You? It was you who built that?' He looked up at the ten-feet-tall rabbit, and then down at her, his eyebrow cocked in suspicion.

A knot of irritation formed in Jody's stomach. Sure, she wasn't Amazonian in height, but she was a respectable five-feet-six and knew her way around scaffolding.

She dropped her unshaken hand to her side. 'Yes, I *sculpted* it. You think I would lie?' She gritted her teeth. What had she been thinking, bringing in this arrogant arse? Worse, using her own money – another act of quiet penance – to do it. Maybe the best idea would be to send him back to London. She'd just have to put her foot down and sort the festival out with an 'it's my way or the highway' speech to the two Mrs Hs. 'Look, Mr Middlemore...'

'Call me Christian.'

'*Mr Middlemore*. I'm sorry to do this to you, but we're no longer in need of an event manager. I'm happy to pay the cost of your transport down here, and reimburse you for time lost, but—'

'You're firing me?' Christian's eyebrows arrowed together in surprise. 'Already? Your online listing sounded desperate. And in your emails you said you were in need of a major bailout, and that if you didn't get an event manager in soon the festival would be a flop. Something's changed?'

Jody focused her gaze on the fairy lights dancing around Mel's Café. Afraid if she glanced up at Christian he'd see the lies in her eyes. 'That's right. Everything is back on track.'

'So, you don't need help finding entertainment?'

'It's sorted.'

'And you've organised parking and how tickets are to be taken.'

A pebble-shaped ball of anxiety formed in Jody's stomach.

'Uh-huh.' She gave a little nod of agreement.

'And you have someone who can work a sound system?'

The pebble began to take on a stone-like quality.

'And the MC has been properly briefed?'

Stone? More like a boulder. A boulder that was making her feel more ill by the second.

'And do you know you've gone quite green? Do you need to sit down? Shall I pop over to that café and get a takeaway cup of tea? A glass of water?'

God, why was he being so concerned? He was being fired. He should be angry with her, not offering to get her a cup of bloody tea.

'You've gone a bit green too, Christian,' Tyler piped up.

'Yeah, and you're sweating,' said Jordan. 'And it's not even that hot. Look, Mum, the edges of his face are all wet.'

Jody snuck a peek at Christian out of the corner of her eye. The boys were right. He did look quite ill. Why? What was she missing?

'I'm fine, boys. It's a rather warm day. However, I do think your mother is being rash sending me back to London without having me check everything over. The festival may be looking in tip-top shape right now, it may even be perfect, but the last thing she or the town needs is a cock-up on the big day.'

Tyler giggled and elbowed Jordan. 'He said "cock-up"!'

Jody closed her eyes and exhaled. Now she was going to be hearing those two words for the next week. Excellent. 'Could you watch your language around my sons, please? They're impressionable. And I promise you, we don't need you. We're fine. In fact, like you said, we're *perfect*.' She angled her chin upwards, defying him to question her one more time.

A screech of anger filled the air. 'You're a mean old cow and I can't believe I ever forgave you for breaking my best crystal vase. Although I do wish I'd been the one to break it… Over your head!'

Christian's lips quirked.

Jody threw her head back and stared at the brilliant blue sky. 'Those women are going to be the death of me,' she muttered before facing Christian again.

Those lush lips of his had gone from quirked to pursed in obvious amusement. Jody itched to clamp her hand over his mouth to hide those twitching lips, the way she did with the boys when they stuck their tongues out or lifted their lips in a sneer.

'Shall I get back in my car, or shall we go and sort things out?' he asked, a smile tugging at the corners of those annoying, I-know-exactly-what-I'm-seeing-and-I-find-it-all-too-hilarious-for-words lips.

Jody paused. An image of the fundraising thermometer she'd painted for the town flickered in the back of her mind. The red 'mercury' was still sitting at next-to-nothing three years later despite her organising six book sales and monthly bingo nights. She might not want Christian Middlemore, but the town needed him if they were going to get the community pool up and running. Up and running? More like totally rebuilt.

'Fine,' she huffed, turning to head back to the hall. 'Follow me. You boys stay out here. You're too young to be exposed to what's going on in there.'

Tyler nodded sagely. 'Cock-ups. Lots of them.'

The clang of what sounded like a chair being thrown against the wall echoed out through the hall's doors.

Christian bent down to the boys' height. 'Do as your mum says. But if you hear screaming, call the police.' He winked and straightened up again.

Jody rolled her eyes. Who did this guy think he was telling her boys what to do? Well, if he tried to tell her what to do, he was going to find out very quickly who was in charge.

* * *

Christian stood beside Jody as she cleared her throat to get the committee's attention. The committee being two women who looked to be in their mid fifties, and who were currently glaring at each other from across the room, an overturned chair between them.

'Christian, I'd like you to meet my fellow committee members. In the left corner we have Marjorie Hunter. Marjorie runs a dairy farm with her husband and their daughter, Serena. Marjorie's also on the committee for the Farmer of the Year Awards.'

16

A soft snort came from the other woman. 'More like the Failure of the Year Awards.'

Jody lifted an eyebrow. 'Shirley.' Her tone was sharp enough to make the woman drop her eyes to the floor.

'Sorry,' she mumbled.

Jody McArthur might look youthful, with her blonde curls bobbing about her shoulders and that spaghetti-strapped sunshine-yellow sundress floating about her tanned and rather firm-looking thighs, Christian noted, but she wasn't to be messed with. Or trifled with. And he got the feeling she wasn't to be flirted with. Which wasn't a problem, not when she had two lust-killers playing outside. He didn't do happy families; he worked. He succeeded. He only ever did his best. *The* best. Anything less was unacceptable.

'And in the right corner we have Shirley Harper. Shirley is an active member of Rabbits Leap. She's raised three sons here. She does a little housekeeping here and there. Volunteers at all the school fundraisers...'

'And thinks she's the Queen of the Leap because one of her sons just happens to be a sporting bigwig.' Marjorie's lip lifted in a sneer directed at her adversary.

'Well, at least he's done something with his life. What's your girl done? Not a lot from what I can gather. Partied a lot. Travelled the globe at someone else's expense. Had to come home and work on the farm because of her fail—'

'Which is where she belongs.' Mrs Hunter cut her off, nostrils flaring in warning. 'There's nothing wrong with admitting you're wrong and that your place is at home. Serena just took some time to come round to the idea. And she's doing great things on the farm. She'll be nominated in the Young Farmer category this year for sure. And she'll win it.'

Was it Christian's imagination or did that last statement lack conviction? He glanced at Jody, who was shaking her head, eyes heavenward. She didn't need a miracle to manage these two. She needed him. Lucky for her, and unfortunately for him, he had nowhere else to be.

'So that's the committee? All of them?' he asked.

'Well, we do get the odd straggler come and sit in and give us their opinion, which we take onboard. The more the merrier. It's a democracy and all that. But we're the core team.'

Christian nodded. 'I see.' Except he didn't. Their festival was being run as a democracy? People wandered in and gave their opinions and expected to be listened to? No wonder Jody had decided to hire an event manager. They didn't need direction, they needed a director. And he was just that.

He squared his shoulders, lifted his chin and marched across the room to where the thrown chair had fallen, set it on its feet and straddled it. 'So, what have you got for me so far? What's pinned down? What needs final confirmation?'

The women glanced at each other. Bottom lips were chomped down on. Arms folded defensively. Eyes faced any which way but his.

18

'Well...' The top of Jody's foot twisted back and forth on the faded oak floors. 'We've had some thoughts. We've contacted a couple of people.'

'And we've got town clearance to use the entire main street,' Mrs Harper added.

'We've *nearly* got town clearance,' Mrs Hunter interjected. 'We've got one holdout. The butcher, John Thompson. He's worried people will be too busy having a good time to bother coming in to buy his meat.'

Mrs Harper tapped the side of her nose. 'I could threaten to reveal to the town that he likes to wear ladies' knickers underneath his butcher's apron.'

'He doesn't!' Mrs Hunter's jaw dropped.

Mrs Harper shrugged. 'I did housework for him a couple of times. He asked me not to do the laundry but I had a few minutes spare and figured I may as well help the man out. Didn't expect to see some rather large lacy numbers in there. I mean, they could've been his wife's, but then he doesn't have one...'

'So, does he know you know?' Mrs Hunter bustled over to the table and picked up her handbag.

'I'm guessing so. Every time he sees me he goes red as a tomato, and he always throws in an extra pack of sausages with the weekly meat order.' Mrs Harper shook her head. 'Not that I'd say anything. It's none of my business what he wears under his trews. And besides, it's nice to know the old grump has a softer side. All that killing and processing of meat could harden a man, I'm sure. It's nice he hasn't let it. Now, shall we go for a cup of tea, Marj? All this planning has left me quite dry.'

'A cup of tea would go down a treat, Shirl. Great idea. Maybe even a scone.'

'With lashings of cream and oodles of jam.' Mrs Harper rubbed her rounded stomach.

Christian couldn't believe what he was seeing. Not two minutes ago the two women had been handbags at dawn, and now they had their arms linked and were off for a spot of tea? And they called that fierce argument a discussion? Who were these people and what had he got himself into?

'Want to come, Jody?' Mrs Hunter called over her shoulder. 'We'll treat the boys to an ice cream.'

'You go on, we'll catch up later. I'll finish briefing Mr Middlemore here.' She waved goodbye to the women and then turned back to Christian. 'So, where were we?'

'We were discussing what's been confirmed for the festival.'

'Oh, yeah, that…' Jody became very interested in the grain of the wooden floors.

Christian's gut twisted. Not a good thing. His gut only twisted when something very bad was going on, when failure was on the horizon. A feeling he'd only felt as bad as this once, at his most recent event, where disaster had struck due to one moment of inattention. His fault completely. And once word got out he'd be a laughing stock. Not just to those in the industry, but to those who were meant to be his nearest and dearest.

This job, this festival, was a way to try and prove to himself he wasn't washed up, that he was still the best. There was no way he was going to bugger it up. Or let anything or *anyone* bugger it up for him. Without his career he had nothing, *was* nothing.

'So just how much *have* you got organised? What's a definite yes?' Jody's face, pink with a mixture of embarrassment and shame, gave him his answer. 'Nothing? Not a single thing?'

'Well, like I said, it's a democracy. But we couldn't decide on anything. Except for Welly-wanging.'

'Welly-wanging?' The narrowing of Jody's nose told Christian he could have sounded more neutral, less disparaging. But really, what the hell was Welly-wanging?

'What's wrong with Welly-wanging?' Her tone was low, deep and dangerous.

Shit. What he would give to wind back the last minute. Still, there was no going back. He had to stand his ground.

'What's wrong with Welly-wanging is that I don't know what it is... But it sounds utterly provincial and I can't imagine people coming to a festival to wang a Welly. Also, it sounds quite filthy, not family-friendly at all.'

Jody's brow furrowed. 'Oh my God. What are you on? It's not dirty, it's throwing a Wellington and whoever throws it the furthest wins a prize.' She shook her head, indignation radiating off her. 'I don't know what you folk from the city get up to so that you think

21

something like Welly-wanging sounds filthy and, quite frankly, I don't want to.'

Christian adopted a calm tone, the opposite to Jody's raised pitch. 'Well even if it's a sweet and innocent game, it doesn't sound all that interesting and it really doesn't seem all that much fun either. There are so many things we could do. Things that will attract people to come rather than repel them.'

'Like what?' Jody took a step towards him, her chin tilted, defiant. 'What would be more fun than throwing a Wellington as far as you can?'

'What wouldn't be? Pony rides. They'd be fun. Amusement park rides. Vintage car displays go down well. What was the idea that sparked this whole festival again?'

Jody's chest rose and fell, a huff escaping her lips. 'The Rabbit Revolt. It's the anniversary of when the town was overrun with rabbits and the local musicians made a deal with the Spirit of the Marsh granting them the ability to play the rabbits away. They marched down the main street, the rabbits followed, and then they were never seen in those numbers ever again. Frankly, I think their playing was probably just terrible and the rabbits ran to save their ears. That'd explain why the local band, The Revolting Rabbits, all descendants of the original musicians, can't play a tuneful note between them.'

An idea sparked in the back of Christian's head. 'There could be something in that tale. But I have a question. What did the musicians have to exchange for the magic of the Marsh Spirit, or whatever it's called…?'

'They had to change the name of the town.'

'From?'

'Arrow's Head.'

'To Rabbits Leap?'

'Yes. But despite much pleading it had to be Rabbits Leap without the apostrophe.'

'I did wonder about the lack of apostrophe. I mean, it could be a statement, "Rabbits Leap", because they do. It's a fact. But it just feels…wrong.'

'Oh, I know. It turns out the Spirit of the Marsh was a trickster who actually quite liked rabbits, but never said no to a deal. So it made us pay by having to explain our choice of apostrophe or lack thereof over and over again for nearly five hundred years.'

'And no one's made a deal since then I take it?'

Jody shook her head, eyes solemn. 'No one's dared.'

'Right. Well, then. We should do a recreation of that event. It could be the grand finale. We could have The Revolting Rabbits play the part of the musicians. The children of the village could dress up as rabbits. We could have a marsh spirit, complete with light show. It would be amazing.'

'But no Welly-wanging.' Jody folded her arms over her chest and tipped her head to the side, eyebrows raised.

'It's not big enough. Not exciting enough. It's a no from me. And my word is final.' Then it hit him… 'You know… Rabbits Leap, no apostrophe, is a little place, but it has a big story to tell... There's a name in that. Do you have a name for the festival yet?'

Jody shook her head.

'Well, how about: The Big Little Festival. It's perfect, don't you think?'

Jody unfolded her arms and placed them squarely on her hips. As much as she appreciated his ideas, his enthusiasm, she hadn't hired him to ride roughshod over their plans, what little there were, for the festival. She'd hired him to work with her, not to take over. Not to steal her opportunity to give back to the community in a meaningful way. And if this was how he ran things, with an iron fist, she was going to have to find another way to give back to Rabbits Leap. 'You know, Christian, what I think is that I can't work under a dictatorship. I think you can call the festival whatever you want, because I quit.'

CHAPTER TWO

Buggery bollocks. Shit. Shit. Shit.

Christian stared at the empty doorway where Jody had stood mere seconds ago. What had just happened? What kind of committee head just quit? And why the hell was she so hung up on this Welly-wanging business?

Still, he stood behind his belief that it wouldn't draw people in, *and* he refused to do anything that would jeopardise the success of The Big Little Festival, or, more importantly, jeopardise what would be left of his career once the pop-star debacle came home to roost square on his head.

Fine. Jody was out. Next step? Go find Mrs Harper and Mrs Hunter and drag them back to the hall to finally nail down some plans. And his say would be final. There would be no democracy under his watch.

He strode across the hall, stepped out into the sunshine and, squinting from its brightness, took in the lay of the land. Total chocolate-box. The kind of town people from overseas expected to see when they came to Devon. All whitewashed stone walls with thatched or tiled roofs. Flower boxes brimming with flowers, and a few weeds. That'd need to be sorted. He mentally began to put together a list of what would have to be done to the village to turn it from sweet and a little sad to something sensational.

Bunting. Lots of it. Criss-crossing the main street. A big sign at either end with The Big Little Festival painted in jaunty colours. They'd need to have portable toilets brought in. They could possibly go at the back of the park. Perhaps with some kind of wall set up to give some privacy and hide their unsightliness.

The street wasn't wide, so he'd have to be economical with the attractions. Which would be what? He stroked his chin, soft spikes reminding him he needed to shave. He was back in the game. He had a job. Now was not the time to look like a down and outer.

A cackle of laughter caught his attention. Mrs Harper and Mrs Hunter. It must be. Another cackle sent him speeding off in its direction towards a building with 'Mel's Café' emblazoned on the window.

He stepped through the door and started at the jolly ting-a-ling of the doorbell. Who had actual bells in their store any more? Where were the electronic chimes? He took in the yesteryear British vibe, all mirrored wall art and china tea trios on display. Had he actually gone back in time? Had Rabbits

Leap decided 1953 was a great year to stop moving forward?

His suspicions deepened when he saw the proprietress. A petite woman with blonde hair, wearing a pink-and-red-rose-covered vintage frock, who was smiling at him in that polite manner that suggested she was wary of the stranger in her café, but would never be rude to a customer.

'Hello? Can I help you?' she asked. 'Would you like to take a seat? Or would you like a moment to take a look at the cabinets?'

'Um, actually, I was just looking…'

'Marjorie.' Mrs Harper's squawk filled the room. 'Look who's tracked us down?! And he's not looking happy… I guess Jody has filled him in on how things are going with the festival.'

'Christian, stop staring at everything like a gormless wonder and sit with us.' Mrs Hunter pushed out a chair and waved at him to join them.

'Can I get you a coffee? Tea? I'm Mel by the way.' The proprietress's smile widened. 'Welcome to Rabbits Leap. I hear you're here to help with the festival.'

Wow, word got around quickly in this place. 'I'm here to do what I can.' Christian attempted to return her smile, but the painful gut-twist had returned. Like a snake intent on wrapping itself into a knot. Many knots. 'An espresso would be great, thanks. Oh, and a scone. Extra cream, please.'

Mel leaned in and whispered conspiratorially, 'They've got you stress-eating already? A word of advice. Just hold your ground. Don't let them boss you about.' She straightened up and sent him on his way with a flick of her hand.

Boss him around? Stress-eating? What did she think he was? A pushover? It would be him doing the bossing. No two ways about that. Christian settled into the chair Mrs Harper had made available for him and gave the women a curt nod. 'Ladies, let's get down to business. The festival is three weeks away. It appears nothing has been organised and time is of the essence. But first things first. Jody has resigned as head of the committee. I shall take her place and this whole democracy thing you've got going on is out the window. There's no time for democracy. Although I'd appreciate your connections within the wider community when it comes to booking entertainment and activities.' Christian nodded in satisfaction and gave the women a tight smile. Job done. They knew the score. They'd be onboard. There'd be no bossing or bulldozing.

A cackle filled the air. High-pitched and hysterical. Followed by the low rumble of a chuckle. They were laughing? At him? He looked over his shoulder to see Mel giving him a pitiful glance. What was going on?

Mrs Hunter was gripping the table and gasping for air. 'Don't tell me,' she panted, as she gasped for air, 'that you said to Jody what you just said to us?'

Mrs Harper was clutching her sides. 'You're hilarious. Who knew the big-city boy would be so very funny? "There's no time for democracy"! Oh my word. Bless your cotton socks, Christian.'

28

'Look, dear.' Mrs Hunter laid her hand on his forearm and gave it a squeeze. 'I don't know how you do things up in London. I'm not even sure what you've done before. Jody didn't say. In fact, hiring you is the only thing she's done without chatting to us about it first, so it's not like we expected you to be here, and we're not entirely sure why we need you in the first place... But you have to understand that trying to tell us how to do things in that stern manner of yours is never going to work. It clearly didn't work with Jody and it doesn't sit well with us.'

Was that a threat he detected in that sweet and low voice? And why had Jody not consulted them? Surely she'd have had to in order to secure the budget for his services? Not that the price had been that high. But he'd needed to get out of town, it was a paying job, and if he made a success of the festival then his great mistake would hopefully be quickly forgotten. His reputation as the best event manager in London would remain intact.

Christian saw something out of the corner of his eye. A young boy with a stick in his hand and a hoop beside him, rolling it down the street. Had he travelled back in time? Was he going mad? Had the stress of the pop-star disaster actually sent him barmy? Was he currently locked up in a padded cell having a delusion?

Two soft thunks and the aroma of rich coffee brought him to his senses.

'Here's your coffee, and the scone, with extra cream. Eat up. Drink up. You've the look of a man whose blood

29

sugar is dropping at a rapid rate.' Mel scooted the sugar bowl his way. 'Pop two of these in, it'll do you good.'

Christian nodded his thanks and spooned the sugar into the coffee, hoping the women across from him, still snickering away, wouldn't notice the trembling of the spoon, or the small granules of sugar that fell onto the table.

'So, how is this going to work then?' he asked. 'Will I make suggestions and you poo-poo them? Will you make suggestions and expect me to action them? Am I to be your lackey?'

'Ooooh, I've always wanted a lackey.' Mrs Harper clapped her hands in delight. 'Yes, I'm very happy with that idea of yours. Excellent idea. You do as we say. I could live with that.'

'Now, now, Shirley.' Mrs Hunter shook her head in mock despair. 'Give the poor lad a break. He's here to help us and he must have connections. Why don't we let him find the musical acts and we can go about telling the Rotary girls what we need for the baking stall. We've got the Welly-wanging sorted; Jody had that well in hand. So that should be it. We're done.'

Christian gripped the coffee cup with both hands, brought it to his lips and sipped, holding the rich and surprisingly delicious liquid in his mouth. Who knew a tiny town could do a better cup of coffee than any he'd had in the city? He swallowed and tried to process what he'd just been told. Did they think a baking stand, some Wellington throwing and a bit of music was all a festival needed? It needed more. Much more.

But it wasn't going to work if he didn't have a team he could trust working with him. Mrs Harper and Mrs Hunter were loose cannons. They'd likely jeopardise plans rather than bring them to fruition. But Jody? There was something about her he felt he could trust. She was determined, yet centred. Solid. She'd make the perfect second-in-command. But she'd quit. *Shit*.

He took another sip of the brain-focusing liquid. No, he wasn't letting these two women smash the career he'd spent his life building into smithereens. He'd left London with his tail between his legs; there was no way he was going back to face the music of his great mistake without a success under his belt. He was going to make this work.

'Ladies.' The word came out with a squeak. Hardly the show of strength he'd hoped for. Still, it had caught their attention. He cleared his throat and tried again. 'Ladies, I appreciate how hard you've worked on this festival. I can see how passionate about it you are. But to be honest, it's not enough. A festival needs to be fun, it needs excitement, amusement, it needs to be something people talk about all year round as they wait for it to come around again. What you've planned is a start. But it's not an end. No. We're going to have to work together to make this bigger. To make it better than any other festival in the area. A festival people from other counties come to visit. We're going to make this festival the biggest little festival in England. Are you with me?'

***

31

'I'm an idiot. More than an idiot. I'm insane. I should be committed.' Jody slapped her hand to her forehead, rubbed it wearily and eyed her brother, who was restocking The Bullion's wine fridge. 'What was I thinking using my...' Jody stopped herself. Tony didn't need to know she'd used her own money to pay for the event manager. If he knew, he'd offer to help her, and she wasn't one to accept offers of help. She'd done everything on her own since the boys came along and being a little out of pocket now wasn't going to change that. 'I can't believe I thought it was a good idea to hire a person who would come in and just destroy everything we'd put together. Well, what little we'd kind of put together...' She eyed the bottles of wine lined up in The Bullion's fridge. Was it too early for a drink? It was after midday, and surely it was five o'clock somewhere in the world. 'Tony, pour your big sister half a glass. I need to take the edge off. And where is bloody Serena? She said she'd meet me here five minutes ago.'

Tony snickered. 'Edge off? You'd need a whole bottle of wine to do that, not just a half glass. I've never seen you so pissed off. And what's five minutes? She probably got stuck in a sheep jam or something. Chill out, Jodes.'

Jody stuck her tongue out at her brother. Then laughed when he stuck his own tongue out and crossed his eyes.

'Seriously? How old are you two? Five?' Serena set her tangerine-coloured tote on the bar with a whump and slid onto the stool next to Jody. 'And why haven't you ordered wine yet? Honestly, what kind of best friend are you? How long have we known each other? You should know by now that if you're demanding I come to a pub then you'd better have something alcoholic ready for me when I get here. And what's the big drama? And who's Mr Fancy Pants? And why do we need to run him out of town, preferably with pitchforks that have sat in hot coals for a couple of hours?'

Jody grinned at her friend. Serena had a way of bringing lightness to even the darkest situations. 'Tony. Did you hear the woman? Wine. Now.' She slapped her hand on the bar for emphasis. 'And bugger the half a glass, make it a whole. Also, could you take some chips up to the boys and tell them they're not to be playing the violent computer games. And if they do they'll lose today's TV privileges. And make sure you impress upon them that if they do play the violent games, *I'll know*. And be sure to raise your eyebrows on the "I know" bit.'

'And they believe you'll know?' Serena grinned.

'They haven't figured out that when I told them I had secret cameras installed upstairs and all around Rabbits Leap to keep an eye on them I was telling them a white lie.'

'Or a blatant lie.' Tony poured the wine into glasses and slid them across the bar. 'I'll go sort out the chips for the boys. Don't steal anything, I have cameras everywhere too, you know.' He winked, and then headed out to the kitchen.

Jody shrugged and lifted the glass to her lips. 'A mum's got to do what a mum's got to do,' she murmured, as much to herself as to Serena. 'Anyway, you won't believe the afternoon I've had. Actually, no, first of all, how are you?'

Serena shook her head. 'I'm fine. Forced into farm slavery. Sick of the smell of cowpats, tired of getting up at the crack of dawn to touch a bunch of udders.' She shuddered. 'But let's not talk about that. Let's talk about you. So, who is this bloke who's got your knickers in a twist? Don't tell me you've finally broken that dumb rule of yours and fallen in love? Don't do it, Jody. Love is a bad thing. Terrible thing. Never ends well. Secure that chastity belt of yours. And double-lock it.'

Jody snorted. 'Thank God I'm not mid glug right now, because you'd be wearing the wine. Nope, he's of no romantic interest to me. No man is. You know that. Not until the boys have left home and no longer need me. What he is, though, is the event manager I hired to help get the festival on track.' She laughed, short and harsh. Regretful. 'On track? He's blown up what few ideas we had. There won't be Welly-wanging.'

'No Welly-wanging? So? What's the big deal about that? It's not like we're known for it. Haven't won any competitions or anything. Heck, didn't Rabbits Leap quit entering them when we came last at our first attempt?'

'Well… I know… But…' Jody twisted her wine glass round and round. 'I don't know. People seem to enjoy it. Families look like they're having a good time…'

She shrugged and traced patterns in the condensation on the wine glass. 'I guess it was a dumb idea. But it was the only idea I was able to get everyone to agree on. I guess it wasn't so much about him saying no to it as the way he said it. He just dismissed it. Wasn't even polite about it. He came in and took over, and well… that's just not the Rabbits Leap way.'

'So, what are you going to do? Get rid of him for hating the one big idea you managed to get past my mother and Mrs Harper? You *did* send him packing, didn't you?' Serena gave her a speculative look. 'You didn't. You *bailed*. You've left him to run the town festival. Jody!' she wailed. 'You can't. We need you. You know how to organise stuff. You've done those bingo nights. Those book sales. The schoolkids were able to go on a trip to the Natural History Museum in London because of your fundraising efforts. But most importantly, we *need* a pool! Sure, it only gets used a couple of months a year. But, oh, what glorious months they are. And if we raise enough we could get some fancy heat-making thing to make the pool swimmable a little longer. I can't believe you let Mr-Fancy-whatever-you-called-him-Pants steamroll you. God, if I meet that man, I'll…'

A cough, of an undeniably awkward nature, stopped Serena in her verbal tracks.

Out of the corner of her eye Jody could see Christian loitering a few feet away. His hands in his shorts pockets. His gaze fixated on the timber beams running across The Bullion's ceiling. Heat rushed to her cheeks.

Serena's eyes widened and her own cheeks flamed. 'He's behind me, isn't he?' she mouthed.

Jody nodded.

'Shit,' she mouthed again and attempted to nonchalantly sip her wine, only to slosh it all over the bar.

'Hey, Christian,' Jody said, but the casual tone came out a croak. 'Are you after a cold drink? Or an alcoholic one? Did Mrs Harper and Mrs Hunter send you round the bend already?'

Christian shifted from foot to foot. Was it her imagination or had his cheeks rouged up? 'Er, no. Not so much. They are…trying…though.'

Serena snorted. 'He just called my mother "trying". Should I throw my wine over him or be happy someone else agrees with me?'

The hint of colour on Christian's cheeks morphed into a full flush. 'Oh God, I'm so sorry. I didn't mean to insult your mother. I didn't know. And if it's any consolation, she's much better than the other one.'

Serena laughed. 'Mrs Harper's a right handful. I don't know how the boys haven't smothered her in her sleep already.'

Jody grinned. 'You forget that Bo's a big-time rugby star, so he's never home. Ridge spends his days and nights with his head under the bonnet of various cars. And Chase… Well, he's the ultimate mama's boy, so he'd be buggered and bereft if anything happened to her.'

'True. Pity she's their mother. Those boys are damn hot. But who'd go there if you had to deal with *that*.'

Christian stepped forward. 'And that's why I'm here. Jody, I need you to come back. I need…' He paused, his Adam's apple bobbing up and down as if something were stuck in his throat and he had to force it out. 'I need your help to deal with, as your friend so eloquently put it, *that*.'

Jody swung round on the stool to face Christian, propped her elbows on the bar, leaned back and laughed. Long and hard. The sound echoed around the bar and caused Christian to take the step he'd taken forward back again. Then another.

Jody sucked in a couple of calming breaths, but couldn't erase the grin that kept returning every time she tried to tame it. 'What happened to Mr-I'm-in-Charge? Mr I'm-the-Boss? Have you finally realised you're not in London any more? That we don't do things down here like you do up there?'

Christian's chest – broad, she noted, and potentially even muscular – rose and fell. Once, twice, three times. He was either trying to keep himself from raging at her for laughing in his face, or breathing to stop himself passing out. Jody noted the grayish-beige tone to his skin and softened. 'Here.' She indicated the stool beside Serena. 'Take a seat. Can I get you a drink?'

'Water.' The corners of his lips lifted in a smile, but his eyes remained unsure. Guarded.

Jody grabbed a pint glass. 'You look like you need a beer. I'm getting you a beer.' She expertly filled the glass and passed it to Christian. Their fingertips grazed against each other as the glass changed hands, sending something that very much resembled a tingle up Jody's arm. Warming the areas it zipped through. Surely not? Her body wasn't *attracted* to him, was it? She brushed the idea aside. No, it was probably just static electricity. She caught Christian's eye and saw her baffled feelings reflected back at her. So, not static electricity then. Strange. Still, Jody mused as she returned to her seat, her body could feel all the tickly thrills it wanted; it didn't mean she was going to do anything about it. Not now, not ever. No amount of lusty body-feels could make up for the pain that followed the inevitable rejection.

'This beer's good. Really good.' Christian ran his tongue over his lips, erasing the foam that had settled there.

Her body started again. The energy moving a little lower, hovering in her stomach, warming what she liked to joke about as the 'cold pit'. *Turncoat*, she scolded. 'It's my brother's. He brews it. He's making a name for himself.'

'He should have a spot at the festival. Did I see a sign for a beer garden?'

Jody nodded.

'Well, it wouldn't be a daft idea to do the beer garden up and make it the official beverage stand. Would he be into that?'

Tony walked through the kitchen doors. 'The boys are sorted with the chips. No violent video games in sight. And would I be interested in what?'

'Tony, this is Christian Middlemore. The new head of the festival committee. He thinks your beer garden would be an excellent addition to the festival. What do you think about that?' Jody raised an eyebrow and prayed her brother would do the loyal family thing and tell Christian to bugger off – even though it was a good idea. One she wished she'd thought of herself.

Tony clapped his hands together with enthusiasm. 'I think that's a fantastic idea. Best idea yet. The beer garden's only just been created, needs a bit of a tidy up, a bit of landscaping and whatnot, but this would give me the excuse I need to pull my finger out of my arse and do it. I'm in.' Tony reached out and grabbed Christian's hand and shook it vigorously.

Traitor, Jody grumbled to herself. That made two backsliders today. Her body and her brother. The two things that were meant to be loyal.

'I'm so glad you like that idea, Tony. I think it could be quite spectacular. I was also thinking you could string lanterns across the area. They'd look brilliant during the day and be a real show-stopper at night for those who choose to stay on after the festival.'

'Great. Love it. I'll get on to it. Jodes? Why didn't we hire this guy earlier?'

Christian took another slurp of beer, set his glass down and focused on Jody. 'Thank you, Tony. I appreciate that you see my worth. If only everyone did. To be honest, I wasn't expecting the committee to be so...' Christian paused, his eyes darting from side to side as if racking his brain for the right word.

'Crazy?' Tony supplied.

'What is with you people today?' Serena snapped, her face lighting up with a grin. 'That's my mother you're talking about!'

'I stand by my statement. I'd also add nutty, forceful, determined and pretty damn intolerable when given a hint of power. I still can't believe you agreed to take those two on, Jodes.' Tony shook his head. 'You must have been having a moment.'

Or desperate to make up for the past. A lump settled in Jody's throat. 'Something like that, Tony. Had myself a wee bit of a turn, obviously.' She forced a smile. 'Anyway, I've quit, so it's not my problem any more.'

'Actually, Jody...' Christian's focus remained on her.

Jody tried not to squirm in her seat. Why did he have to keep looking at her so intently? And why did he have to have those warm, roasted chestnut-coloured eyes that could melt steel, or an ice maiden's vow to herself. Ugh. She folded her arms and pinched the soft undersides in an attempt to pull herself together.

'...I wasn't joking when I said I needed your help. I do. And I hate admitting that. But Rabbits Leap is different to what I'm used to. The people here are set in their ways. And there seems to be some sort of hierarchy I can't figure out. Well, I can. At the moment it seems the locals are on top and I'm at the bottom of the pile. Which would be fine, but I need to make this work. I need someone to help me figure this place and its people out. I need you, Jody. I want *you.*'

Serena giggled. 'Well, that's not the kind of declaration a girl hears every day. I think I'd better leave you two alone.' She slugged back the dregs of her wine, gathered up her bag and winked at Jody. 'Have fun!'

Frustrated, Jody lowered her head into her hands and sank her teeth into her lower lip. What choice did she have? If she said no, she'd be stuck in the same place she'd been for years – looking for a way to make up for her one night of recklessness that had impacted on so many. But if she said yes? She recalled those flickers of electricity that had danced over her skin when they'd touched. If she said yes, she'd be putting herself in a position she'd sworn never to be in. She'd be opening herself up to attraction. Which could lead to desire. And then the ultimate no-no: love. And, in her experience, that never led anywhere good.

'We need to get something clear,' she mumbled into her hands. 'You are not my favourite person right now. But I'll work with you. Not because I want to, but because I don't want this little town to lose its one big dream. So I'll come back onboard, but you need to understand that I won't be dictated to. If we're butting

41

heads, we'll have to find someone for a swing vote. Understood?'

Christian lifted his head a little, just enough so one half of his face was in view. 'Mr Fancy Pants understands.' He gave her a cheeky grin.

Her heart must have discovered a trampoline in her chest because it did a flip-flop. Jody closed her eyes against that far-too-cute smile. It was too late to back out. She'd done the deal. But why did she suspect the price she'd pay would be high?

CHAPTER THREE

Focus.

Christian forced himself to read the words on the laptop, but for the first time in a long time the screes of plans and ideas he had for an event held little to no interest. Not when his mind was filled with images of curling blonde hair that bounced on sun-kissed shoulders, tanned legs so long they looked like they could give The Shard a run for its money, and the tantalising hint of divinely curved breasts.

Damn it! The last thing he needed was to have the hots for a woman he was supposed to be working with. The building blocks to success did not include romance. He'd learnt that time and time again when his previous attempts at relationships had gone south; when his girlfriends began to put pressure on him to cut back on the hours he spent at work so they could spend more time together. Further proving his suspicion that having both fairy tale-style love and a career was impossible. The only compromise was partnership, two people supporting each other to further each other's success. An arrangement his parents had down pat. A united front at work functions. But behind the door of their family home? Short, sharp and dismissive summed it up. The only time kind words were exchanged was when a goal was met. A win had. It was the only way he'd received any attention. Not that his decision to go into event management was taken seriously by them. No doubt when his recent failure became public knowledge they'd pop open a bottle of champagne…

He pulled up a budgeting template and pushed the self-pity away. Self-pity was not what winners were made of. And even though he'd not followed the family into law or medicine as expected, he'd still become the best in his field. And he wasn't going to let one stupid error derail everything he'd built.

A scuffle outside his bedroom door caught his attention.

'You're a cock-up,' a voice yelled.

'No, you are. Your face is a cock-up.' The retaliation was met with another round of scuffling.

What the hell was going on out there? Why was Tony allowing people to fight in his establishment? When Jody had mentioned his accommodation she'd assured him that, despite its being above a pub, it wouldn't be rowdy.

'Boys. Do I need to hide your tablet again?' The stern warning put a stop to the fighting.

Three sharp raps on his door followed. Shit, Jody was here to see him. He peered at the time on the laptop. Of course she was, they had a meeting. Which she'd brought her sons to. Something she'd not mentioned and something he couldn't condone. If he'd wanted to work with kids he'd have been a teacher.

He marched to the door, his head full of rebukes, pulled it open, and all his words of chastisement disappeared as the air whooshed from his stomach at the sight before him. Jody's two young lads, with those matching sandy-blond curls, mischievous grins and knobbly knees peeping out below denim cut-offs, were smiling up at their mum with absolute adoration as she ruffled their curls. Her smile as big as theirs, with every bit as much love. This was what he'd always imagined a family would be like. A proper family. Love, laughter, teasing. Not cold, distant and perfunctory.

Jody looked up in surprise. 'Oh, that was quick. I've only just knocked.'

'Well, I could've heard you coming from two towns away.' Christian swung the door open all the way and indicated for them to come in. 'You didn't tell me you were bringing them.'

'"Them" have names. Tyler, Jordan, you remember Christian.'

The boys glared at him with open hostility. 'He ruined our fun.' Tyler narrowed his eyes.

'Yeah. We were having a good time until he yelled at us.' Jordan scratched at a scab on his elbow. 'How did he not know it was a slide anyway? For an adult that's pretty dumb.'

A pretty flush of pink hit Jody's cheeks. 'Sorry about these two. You'll get used to them.'

Get used to them? What? Christian shut the door behind them. 'Um, what do you mean, "get used to them"? They're not going to be coming with you to all our meetings, are they?'

Jody nodded. 'Sure they are. We're a package deal. They go where I go.'

'But that's hardly professional.' The gentle rhythmic thud of Christian's heart began to pick up pace. This wasn't how business was done. How was he going to ensure the festival went off without a hitch with two young people getting in the middle of things? And if the festival didn't go off without a hitch? Goodbye career, hello humble pie.

'You want me. You want my family.' Jody's hands left the boys' shoulders and flew to her hips, her chin tilted. 'The boys and I are a unit. We stick together. Also, there's no one to take care of them.'

'What about your brother? Or your friend I met earlier?' Christian had a feeling he was clutching at straws, but wasn't giving up easily.

'Tony has The Bullion to run. His fiancée, Mel, helps him when she's not running her café. Serena is on the farm most of the day and, frankly, I don't know that she's responsible enough to handle the two boys. She'd probably take them on a ramble and lose them.'

'Your mum? Your dad? Their dad?' Christian sank onto his bed as the world began to tip a little sideways. Was the room too small for four people? Because it felt like he was losing oxygen.

'My mum passed away when I was five. My father passed away not long ago. And, their father is... Not on the scene.' The last four words were soft, but there was no missing the steely tone. The boys' father was not a topic up for discussion when the boys were around.

Christian ran his hand through his hair. 'Okay, so they're coming with us.' He turned his gaze on the boys. 'We're going to have to set some rules, though. If your mother or I are talking to an adult, you can't interrupt. And you can't get rowdy like you were out in the corridor. Consider yourself Rabbits Leap ambassadors. Pretend you're fine, upstanding young men...or something.'

'Pretend?' Jody frowned, but a smirk threatened to ruin her act.

'Fine.' Christian grinned. 'Act like the fine, upstanding young men I know you to be. And no saying "cock-up". At least not within the earshot of adults.'

'Yes, sir,' the boys chorused, saluting Christian. Their little faces solemn, their eyes glinting with good humour.

Christian fought the urge to reach out and ruffle their hair as Jody had done earlier. They were good kids. But it was better he kept his distance. Rabbits Leap was only a pit stop until he was sure things were going to blow over back home. There was no point forming attachments. Especially as he was incapable of living up to any 'attachments' expectations.

'I was also thinking they'd be quite good if we do end up needing a swing vote.' Jody leaned against the windowsill.

'But there's two of them? What if they can't agree? And do we really want to put the decisions in the hands of, what…a couple of eight-year-olds?'

'Hey! We're nine.' Jordan stamped his foot and folded his arms across his chest.

'Sorry. Nine-year-olds then.' Christian nodded an apology to Jordan and Tyler, then looked over at Jody. 'But really? We have to take this seriously.'

'I am. This is a family festival. It's for people of all ages. And who knows better what kids like than kids? Besides, they rarely disagree on anything. And if they do we'll flip a coin. Or we'll get Mrs Harper's opinion.'

Christian's heart broke out into another trot. 'No, no need to get Mrs Harper involved. We'll flip a coin.'

Jody's smirk blossomed into a grin, one that revealed a cute dimple on her left cheek. What would it be like to touch, to kiss? The thought rose unbidden. What the hell was going on with him?

Christian leapt off the bed. Now was not the time to be thinking amorous thoughts. Now was the time to work. He could think amorous thoughts another time, about another woman. *Definitely* another woman. One not so obviously family-focused. One who would understand that work and winning came first. 'Look, this room is no place for a meeting. It's small. Cramped.' And feeling more cramped by the second as he realised that Jody's white paint-spattered tank top was ever so slightly see-through, revealing a hint of her bra. Lacy, latte-coloured. And housing two things he really shouldn't be thinking about. 'We need to get out, now.' He charged for the door and made his way down the hallway, down the stairs and into The Bullion's dining area, only knowing he was being followed because of the bang of his bedroom door closing, followed by multiple thumps of feet on floorboards closing in behind him.

What the heck had just gone on? Jody pondered as she stared at Christian's back, which wasn't so much taking the lead as beating some kind of retreat. One minute they were discussing the boys' involvement, the next he'd bounded off the bed and bolted from the room.

But there had been a moment before that. A moment she thought she'd imagined. Or perhaps wanted to imagine. His eyes had flicked down, lingered on her top. Her chest. Then his eyes had widened, and he'd been up and gone. A man on a mission. Or a man looking to escape whatever was on his mind.

And what had been on his mind? Her? Jody glanced down at her top and saw it through new eyes. A man's eyes. Oh. Her old painting tank top was a little see-through. And her bra was perhaps a little alluring.

49

Not that she was trying to lure anyone with it. It was just there to hold up her boobs.

A shiver trailed its way down her spine. Why did she suddenly feel as if she'd exposed herself to Christian? Why hadn't she brought another top in case it got chilly? Because it was summer. A warmer than usual summer at that. And why did she have a feeling things were only going to get hotter? Jody clenched her jaw. Nope. No heat here. Nothing steamy at all.

She followed the boys into the dining room and looked for the iced-water pitcher Tony always had filled and ready for customers. What she needed to do was drench herself in that, cool off... And give Christian a view of everything? Wet T-shirt competition style? No. No water. She just needed to continue ignoring the fact that he was the hottest man she'd seen in years, while continuing to remember her numberone rule. No. Men. Allowed. Not until her boys were men. That was her rule and she was sticking with it.

And then what? The shiver returned, needling her conscience. And then what? Then she'd find another excuse, another way to keep her heart locked up, wrapped in chains and buried down a concrete-filled well.

'Mum.' Tyler tugged at her hand. 'Where is Christian going?'

Jody gripped Tyler's hand. Her boys were what mattered. They needed to grow up knowing they were all that mattered to her. They weren't to feel like a second thought, the way she had growing up. She gave Tyler's hand a squeeze. 'No idea, T. Let's follow him and find out, shall we?'

The three of them picked up their pace as they half walked, half ran after Christian, who was storming down the main street, head down, shoulders hunched. He stalked past the butcher's, passed Mel's Café, didn't look twice at the village hall, and continued up towards the school.

Her arms began to ache and she looked down to see the boys lagging behind her. Their chests heaving with exertion. 'Christian!' she called. 'You've got to slow down. Our legs aren't as long as yours!'

'Nearly there,' he yelled back.

To her relief he began to slow down. Then stopped. In front of the old pool, she realised.

'Come on, boys, we might as well see what this madman is up to.' They traipsed over to where Christian was standing, his eyes trained on the mural painted on the brick wall that separated the pool from the community.

'Do you like it?' asked Jody as she took in the picture she knew like the back of her hand. A fifty-by-ten-feet painting, filled with images of the Leap, from the town's oldest resident, Mr Muir, hunched over his daily crossword, to a younger, laughing Mrs Harper washing a shopfront window, to her own boys frolicking in the pool – not that they'd had the opportunity as it had been out of commission well before they were born. The lives of the local residents

51

were backed by the rolling Rabbits Leap hills, criss-crossed with hedgerows and stone walls, and a clear blue sky. She considered it her greatest work. And hoped one day, once the boys were older, she'd be able to work seriously on her art. Take on commissions. Make enough money to realise the one dream she'd had before the boys were born: to travel through Europe seeing her favourite works of art in the flesh, not on some computer screen or in the pages of a coffee-table book.

'It's great. The artist really captured the boys. Their light. Their happiness. Their joy. You can almost feel the coolness of the water. I can see the wisdom coming from that gentleman. And Mrs Harper's raucous joy. The artist is talented.' He pulled his phone out of his pocket and took a picture of the mural.

'The artist is me,' said Jody. The words came out more shyly than she'd hoped for.

'Wow, a sculptress and a painter. You really are very talented. Do you do it for a living?'

Jody shook her head. 'No. It's just something I do when I have some spare time. Looking after the boys and the day-to-day work on the farm keep me busy enough.'

'You're a farmer too? Like Serena?' Christian's lips quirked in disbelief.

Jody refrained from rolling her eyes. 'Yes, I'm a farmer. Sort of. It was my grandparents' farm and it was left to me when they passed away. Except I don't know all that much about farming, so I've a farm hand, Jack. He does the hard work. I tend to do more of the managerial side of things. Not that I know much about managing anything, but it seems the story of my life is being plunged into a deep pool and being told I can sink or swim.'

Christian's eyes darted between the two boys. 'Well, it seems you're very good at swimming.'

'I could be better. It'd be nice for the farm to make enough money to not just pay Jack and the household bills, but for the boys and I to go on holidays. Do more than meander around this place. Still, I can't complain. We've a roof over our heads and enough coming in that we're fed and clothed.'

Christian's eyes flicked down, then quickly up. Jody crossed her arms over her chest and wished she'd sprung for a better-quality tank top, preferably made of inch-thick opaque material.

Christian, as if sensing her discomfort, changed the subject. 'So, now we're out of that tiny, cramped space and at the source of inspiration to remind us why we're going to make the festival a runaway success, let's brainstorm. Let's combine ideas. Work out what we can do with the space and time available, then get the rest of the committee to secure what we need.'

'Well, I really liked the idea of replicating the Rabbit Revolt. I could design the costumes. There's a local group that are keen on sewing, the Stitch 'n' Snitch club. They come together every week to sew.

And gossip. Mostly gossip,' Jody admitted. 'We could get them to whip up the costumes. And, like you suggested, the local kids could play the rabbits.'

'Mum!?' Tyler wailed. 'It's school holidays. That sounds like we have to take part in a school play.'

'And I hate taking part in plays,' Jordan moaned. 'They always make me be a statue of some sort.'

'Because you can't remember your lines,' Tyler snickered.

'Shut up, Tyler. At least I didn't have to dance with a girl like you did in the last one.'

'Yeah, that was gross.' Tyler stuck his tongue out and faux-gagged. 'I'm not dancing with girls at the festival. Okay?'

Christian regarded the boys seriously. 'So, if we don't have dancing, you're in? And you think the rest of the local kids will get onboard?'

Unexpected warmth flooded Jody. It was good to see the boys interacting with a man on a man-to-man level. They didn't get that a lot. Tony was always busy, and her farm worker, Jack, was always out in the fields, so their role models were few and far between. A fist tightened around her heart as guilt niggled at her. Would her refusal to give a relationship a chance, to get close to another man, mean they were missing out on something special?

'We'll get them onboard. We'll remind them it's for the pool and how cool it would be to have bombing competitions once it's opened.' Jordan stuck his hand out. 'So it's a deal.'

The niggle deepened as Jody watched the boys and Christian solemnly shake hands all round. Christian showing them how in an authoritative manner. Why hadn't she thought to teach them to shake hands like that? They'd be out in the real world one day and if they had wet-fish handshakes no one would take them seriously. She pushed the guilt away. It wasn't going to help matters, and besides, this wasn't about them or her, this was about making amends to the community. In a super-secret, stealth manner.

'Right.' She cleared her throat. 'So that's sorted. What else can we do to ensure this is the festival to end all festivals? A Ferris wheel? A carousel?'

Christian looked up from tapping on his phone. 'All good ideas. But we need to remember there's only so much space.' He stroked his chin thoughtfully. 'Hmmm, we're surrounded by hills, and farms, and it's a fundraiser for a pool. I feel there's something there...' He gazed off into the distance. 'I've got it! We could do a giant slip and slide and create one of those makeshift pools using hay bales. People would love it! People could pay for, say, a thirty-minute swim and they could pay per slide. Can't you just imagine it? They'd come from all over to have a swim and a slide. Hell, we could try and make it a world-record thing. The world's longest slip and slide.'

Jody found herself nodding enthusiastically. 'That could be cool. Really cool. And maybe, if we do go for the record, the local news might pick it up and that could bring us some promotion.'

'Local news? Oh no, let's go regional. No, national. Why do a little when you can do a lot. More is more, Jody. More is more.'

Christian dropped down onto the grass, then grabbed her hand and pulled her down beside him. Close. Their knees brushed and those volts of energy surged, up her thigh, straight to the area she'd purposefully ignored for the last decade. She inched her knee away, and then pulled her hand out of Christian's, ignoring how empty it suddenly felt. And how perfect it had felt being held by a strong and capable hand, as opposed to two soft young ones.

'Jody, this wonderful mural of yours needs to have the people of Rabbits Leap milling in front of it every summer as they wait for the pool to open. And I think the water theme combined with the anniversary of the eviction of the rabbits is going to take this little festival of yours to the next level.'

'Well, then. Let's do it! Let's make it happen.' Jody paused, uncertainty coiled in her belly. 'Um, Christian? How are we going to make this happen?'

Christian threw his head back and laughed. Deep, chocolatey. Sexy too.

Stop perving. He'll leave. They always do, one way or the other. You don't need that kind of rejection.

'And that, Jody, is why the town hired me. I can make it happen. You might need to point me in the direction of a farmer who does the old square hay bales as opposed to the round ones. But the rest? I can

56

sort the rest. Just you watch. That's what Rabbits Leap's paying me for.'

The uncertainty evaporated, only to be replaced with the urge to tell Christian the truth about his coming to Rabbits Leap. 'Christian. Can you keep a secret?'

Christian angled his head and gave her a curious glance. 'I can be the soul of discretion.'

She leant in, motioned for him to do the same, and whispered, 'The town isn't paying for you to be here. I am.'

Christian's jaw dropped, revealing perfectly even, nicely spaced, white teeth. Was there anything imperfect about this man? And why was she thinking about his teeth and general good-lookingness when she'd just told him the truth about his employment?

'But why? Why you? Why not the town?'

Jody sighed. She couldn't tell him the whole truth. She was too ashamed. But she could skirt around it. 'The thing is, Christian, this town has been good to me. When my mother passed away they organised the funeral because my father was in no way capable of doing so. He was pretty much in denial and just set about running the pub as if nothing had happened. Over those months the women of Rabbits Leap were always bringing stews and pies, hand-me-down clothes, anything they thought Tony and I might need. In their own way, and alongside my grandparents, they helped raise us until I got to be older and became self-sufficient enough that I could care for Tony and myself.' She pulled at the grass, threw the tufts aside, tugged at it some more. 'When the boys came along they helped me as much as I'd let them. Showed me how to change a nappy, how to bathe them. When mastitis hit, they saw the signs early enough and ensured I was taken care of. And again there was the food and the hand-me-downs. Apparently nobody throws anything away in this town. Even now, the boys are wearing clothing that belonged to Mrs Harper's sons.' She brought her knees up to her chest in a hug and looked up into the hills, lush green with swathes of gold where the rape fields bloomed. 'So when they asked me to take on the festival, I said yes. Without hesitation. I owe this town so much. I owe them the good life I've lived. It could've so easily gone the other way.'

'So, when you realised wrangling with the two Mrs Hs wasn't going to plan and things were going nowhere fast, you called me in.' Christian nodded in understanding. 'Well, I'm glad you did. I have a feeling I'm going to enjoy this project, very much.' He flashed her another smile. The wide-mouthed open kind that made Jody glad she was sitting because her knees probably couldn't have held her up had she been standing.

Another time, another place, another situation, and she could have quite liked Christian. More than liked him. But she had her vow to keep and two young boys to grow into fine young men before she could bother with that side of things. And after that? She'd be safe. She wouldn't need to use the boys as an excuse to keep relationships at bay, because there was no one in Rabbits Leap who'd ever caught her eye, and Christian would be going back to London, well out of temptation's way.

Still, as the sun glinted off his artfully styled brown hair, his eyes sparkling with excitement, she couldn't help but think *what if?*

CHAPTER FOUR

Christian took a sip of his flat white and slumped back in the café's retro metal-framed, cherry-coloured wooden chair, the milky, earthy liquid soothing the confusion jangling his thought processes. For a second outside the old pool he'd felt a connection with Jody. And not because they'd reached some sort of truce, and decided to stop fighting each other. It had been different. The kind of connection you feel when your eyes meet your date's over a few glasses of something alcoholic at a bar. Or when you've gone out with a woman a few times and it's time to take things to the next level. And you both want to.

Except he didn't want to. Even if some chemical part of him did. Jody was beautiful and clearly talented, but there was the matter of the boys, who were currently sitting to the left of him, their twin heads bowed towards a tablet screen as they tap-tap-tapped on some game. They weren't part of his life plan. He didn't think it would be fair to raise a child in an environment where work and winning came first. Sure, he'd survived. Just.

He'd been forced to grow from a shy and awkward boy to a strong man who others paid attention to, listened to, and were happy to take orders from. Well, apart from the older festival committee members of Rabbits Leap. But he'd sort them out soon enough. Yes, his home environment had brought success, but deep in his gut he suspected there were other, better ways to raise a family. Ways he knew nothing of, and didn't have the role models to learn from.

'So, we're all good then?' Jody looked up from the serviette she'd scribbled notes on. 'We've got the ideas for festival activities down, so now we just have to decide what people will find more enjoyable, and I'm sorry, Christian, but I just don't think food trucks will fly when compared to one of our baking stalls. We've some master bakers here, and you've tried Mel's scones. Who wouldn't want one of those?'

Christian eyed the crumbs left on his plate. 'They're delicious, don't get me wrong, but while you locals trust the baking here, home-baked goods might not appeal to outsiders. I mean, who knows what conditions they're cooked in? What if a fly landed in a batch of biscuit mix?'

Jody groaned. 'Oh, for Pete's sake. Really? How likely do you think that is to happen?'

'I bet you it has, somewhere. All I'm saying is a little variety could be good. There's a fair happening a few towns over that's advertising food trucks. Indian, Mexican, Greek. I mean, who doesn't love a good souvlaki? Or a tasty taco?'

Jody's answer came in the form of a squeak and rumble from the direction of her stomach. 'Traitor. I knew I should've gone for a scone *and* a sausage roll.' She grimaced as she rubbed it. 'I suppose there's nothing wrong in at least checking out the offerings. Maybe we could do both? Food trucks and baking?'

'Perhaps.' Christian diarised a trip to the fair on his mobile. 'But it all comes down to space. We've only a smallish amount to work with and we need to maximise it as much as possible. It is The Big Little Festival, after all. It needs to go off with a bang.'

'So, I guess that means we can't do both the carousel and the Ferris wheel, or the vintage car show and the jumble and book sale.' Jody spooned sugar into her coffee and gave it a swirl.

'Perhaps we can. The jumble and book sale could be held in the hall. I'm having second thoughts on the vintage car show. Too big, and it won't bring in money. You know, we could do some really old-fashioned style festival activities. It would be in keeping with the old-time feel of this place. Say a ring toss, or a kissing booth, even.'

Jordan's head lifted. 'Just don't you be the one kissing, Mum. We'd make no money.'

Jody swatted Jordan's head. 'Oh, you shush, cheeky boy.'

'I don't know, Jordan. I can imagine there'd be a couple of people out there who'd pay to be kissed by your mum. I'd be first in line.' Christian paused as Jody flushed bright red, then realised how what he'd said sounded. 'You know, just to get the ball rolling...'

'I'm not kissing anyone,' she croaked. 'The kissing booth isn't happening. Besides, germs.'

'Good point, Mum. Everyone knows girls have lots of germs.' Jordan nodded his approval and returned to the screen.

Christian suppressed a laugh. Even choked up and embarrassed, Jody was hot. And even though he had no intention of pursuing anything with her, he couldn't help but wonder if she had a partner. Earlier, when he'd grabbed her hand and their knees had touched, she'd acted like he'd bitten her. Or jolted her with a taser. Whatever had passed between them sure had some electricity behind it. And while he didn't want to explore that connection, he wasn't sure why Jody was so keen to shut it down? Was there someone in the picture, secreted away on the side? Did she not want the boys to see her with another man unless it was serious?

'Christian? You in there? What else would you suggest we add to the programme?'

'Pony rides, like we talked about. A rural petting zoo perhaps. All easily doable. But of course it's not going to happen unless you get sign-off on using the main street. We were waiting on one person, weren't we? The butcher? He had to give his okay along with all the other business owners to host the festival on the main street?'

Jody nodded. 'Yeah, but he's adamant it'll hurt his business. Won't budge.'

'But we have something on him, don't we? We could do what Shirley suggested and use that to get what we want, couldn't we?' Christian pressed.

'Oh no.' Jody shook her head, eyes wide in horror. 'We couldn't do that. It wouldn't be right.'

Christian admired her integrity, but they weren't getting the festival off the ground without each and every business owner's consent. 'Sorry, Jody, I disagree. What's not right is halting the progress and growth of this village because you're afraid you might sell a few less lamb chops one day of the year. I'm going to chat to him, now.' He scraped the chair back and stood up.

'If you're doing that, I'm coming with you. I won't have you upsetting a member of this town unnecessarily. Boys, you stay here. Stay out of trouble. I'll be back in ten minutes.'

'I'll say what needs to be said, nothing more. Besides, there's more than one way to get what you want. I just need to find out what's important to him. What he wants. I'm sure I won't have to resort to revealing his secret to the whole village.' Christian marched through the door and into the street, quiet apart from a dog tied up outside the café, staring longingly at a cat lazing in the sun across the road.

There was a tug on his shirt.

'You are *not* going to tell him you know he wears lacy underwear,' Jody whispered. 'It's not your business. It's nobody's business. And what if he digs his heels in deeper? Christian, if he knows Mrs Harper has been spreading rumours about him, you could start some sort of town war.' Jody spun him round to face her. 'This isn't London. If you have a falling out with someone, you're going to have to see them again. A lot. You can't do this.'

'I'll do what needs to be done.' Christian shrugged her off, strode across the road and paused in front of the butchery – 'Stripped and Fed'. What the hell kind of name was that for a butchery? Graphic much? And now he was going to have to meet the proprietor, knowing that when he stripped he was in lacy knicks. Bloody hell. If he didn't need this job so much he would have been out of here in five seconds flat.

He pushed open the door and was greeted by refreshing chilled air, and the earthy, metallic scent butcheries exuded. He breathed it in. There was more to that scent, though. There was a hint of spiciness too. Before him, display fridges were filled with choice cuts, gleaming pink and red. He glanced up and saw fat-speckled salami hanging. Different widths, different lengths, and from the looks of it, different varieties. At the end of the room another fridge displayed prosciutto, pre-cut salami, pancetta and coppa, as well as cheeses, olives and sun-dried tomatoes. He strolled over for a closer look. Not just any cheese, a range of goat's cheese – chèvre, brie, blue. Sitting alongside those were camembert, gouda, cheddar, with a sign stating all products were produced locally. This wasn't a butchery, it was foodie heaven. An idea occurred to him...

Jody burst through the door, her eyes wild with panic. 'Where's Mr Thompson?' She craned her neck over the meat-filled fridges. 'Don't tell me he's stormed off in a rage.' She gnawed at her lower lip. 'What have you done, Christian?'

'I've done nothing. But I have a way to get what we want.'

'Done? Who's done what?' A tall, burly man clomped his way towards them. White boots slapping on the tiled floor.

'Mr Thompson!' Jody squeaked. 'We were wondering where you were…'

Christian grabbed Jody's hand and gave it a squeeze, hoping it would convey she could trust him. That he wasn't going to blow it. She snatched it away and shoved her hands into the pockets of her denim shorts.

'Finally, I get to meet the great Mr Thompson. It's an absolute pleasure, sir.' Christian offered his hand to Mr Thompson, who looked at it with suspicion. Christian dropped his hand. Maybe this wasn't going to be as easy a sell as he'd thought. He cleared his throat. 'Right, so, um, as much as I'd like to make this a social occasion, Jody and I are here on business. I hear you're refusing to give the okay for the festival to take place in the main street.'

'It'll ruin a day's takings.' Mr Thompson picked up a knife and steel from his butcher's block and began to sharpen it vigorously. 'I don't know who you are, but if you knew anything about Rabbits Leap, you'd know it's not the kind of place where a person can afford to lose a day's takings.'

'I understand that, Mr Thompson, I do. But it's imperative you give us the okay today. The festival is just under three weeks away. Tickets have been sold, in fact they've sold out.' The fib rolled off his tongue. Sometimes you had to expand on the truth to get what you wanted. 'And if we don't hold it here, we'll have to beg a farmer to lease us some land. An expense we were hoping to avoid, as we're aiming to raise enough money to revitalise the community pool.'

'You mean the community pool I've never swum in and am not likely to. So why should I care?' A slab of eye fillet was slapped on the block and sliced efficiently.

'Look, here's what I'm proposing. You give us the okay and we...'

Something warm and soft gripped his hand, squeezed it. Jody's hand. Did she really think he was going to resort to blackmail? The idea was tempting, but you didn't get anywhere with people by screwing them down with threats. You just had to make them see why your way was better.

'The thing is, you're going to give us the go-ahead to hold the festival, and we're going to ensure you get top billing as a business supporter of the festival on the brochure all festivalgoers will be given on arrival. We'll also ensure social media posts promote Stripped and Fed.' Christian noted the raising of the butcher's eyebrows, the slight cocking of his head. The fish was on the hook. Now to reel it in. 'Once people see you're more than a butchery, that you've delectable deli goods as well, you'll make more than your day's takings. You'll make it three times over.'

'Four times over,' Jody added with an affirmative nod. 'Maybe more. And once people taste those cheeses and meats of yours, they'll return from towns all over to buy them again. They're that good.'

'Well, I know that.' Mr Thompson grunted 'The love and care I put into each batch ensures every product is top-notch.'

'Well, it's time the rest of the county knew that too. And this is the ideal way to do it. So, do we have your permission?'

Mr Thompson raised his knife and gave it a threatening shake. 'You'd better make me a rich man, even if only for one day.'

'Thank you, Mr Thompson. You're the best. Who knew underneath that tough exterior was such a big softy.' A blush of pink appeared on Jody's cheeks. Christian bit back a laugh. The butcher's nostrils flared in suspicion as his hand gripped the knife tight enough to reveal big, meaty knuckles.

He pulled Jody back a step, then another, until their backs had reached the door. 'Right, that's settled. We'll be going. Nice to meet you. Bye.' He yanked open the door, stumbled out onto the street, and ran hand in hand with Jody back towards Mel's Café, only stopping when they reached its front door.

***

Jody swung to face Christian. 'Why didn't you tell me you weren't going to blackmail him?' she demanded.

He shrugged. 'I tried to. I squeezed your hand, remember? That was me saying "trust me, I've got this".'

'I thought it was you telling me not to interfere.'

'Isn't that the same thing?' A smirk appeared on his lips. 'And anyway, at the end there, you very nearly did interfere. That man knew something was up. And for one scary minute I thought we were about to be made into mincemeat.'

Laughter bubbled up in Jody's chest. 'Or whizzed up into smoked liver pâté.' Christian blurred before her as tears of laughter sprang to her eyes. 'Can you imagine? We could have become one of his special deals for the week. No one would suspect a thing. We'd be dead meat. Literally.' She swiped away the trail of tears making their way down her cheeks, and rubbed the tears from her eyes, only to see Christian bright red with contained mirth. His own eyes swimming with unshed tears.

'Oh God. And our bones would have been sold off to the farmers for their dogs to gnaw on, or we'd have ended up in a pot and turned into gourmet stock for him to sell alongside stewing meats.' A bellow escaped his lips, followed by another.

Jody's attempt at pulling herself together fell completely apart and, next thing she knew, they'd collapsed on the pavement. Their shoulders pressed together in mutual support as they cackled.

When her abs were aching, her shoulders had stopped shaking and the tears had slackened off from a torrent to a dribble, she tilted her head up and inhaled the fresh, sun-warmed air. Her hand felt hot and tight and she glanced down to see that, all this time, it had been clutching Christian's. Fused even. As if against her will it had chosen to stay interlocked with his hand, happy as a magnet that had found a pole that clicked. Her hand had betrayed her and forgotten her number one rule. No men allowed.

She dared to sneak a look at Christian. He'd gone as still as she had. His brow creased. A look she couldn't place in his eyes. Confusion? Worry? Surprise?

He gave her a gentle nudge. 'Why didn't you tell me the butcher was more than just your usual small-town butcher? The man's making products that, if cheesageddon or deli meatageddon ever happened, people would sell their first-born children for. Heck, they'd sell their souls.'

'How do you know they're that good? You haven't even tried them?' Jody flicked her gaze down to their hands. Still interlaced. Still together. Why hadn't she remedied that problem yet?

'I guess I didn't even have to taste them to know they'd be good. They had that look about them, you know? That look that tells you if something's going to work or not.'

Jody's heart, only minutes earlier thumping at a rapid rate of BPMs, stalled as their eyes locked. The distant buzz of a chainsaw became a hum, the sparrows chirping in the trees faded into an unmelodic tune of blips and bleeps. The balmy breeze picked up, whipping tendrils of hair in front of Jody's face. She watched, mesmerised, as Christian's hand moved towards that hair in slow motion, his eyes not leaving hers. He swept the locks gently to the side of her face and tucked them behind her ear, his fingers tracing the delicate skin of her ear down to the lobe, where they stopped, his thumb stroking the tender piece of flesh, sending piercing quivers straight to her lower stomach, causing liquid heat to pool.

'Yeah, I think I know what you mean,' she said, nodding, and somehow that nod morphed into a slight angling of her head, and a tiny tip forward. As if her lips were betraying her along with that hand. Was it her imagination or was Christian getting closer? Out of focus. Hell, he was disappearing altogether. Why was she closing her eyes?

'Mum. You're holding Christian's hand. Do you two like each other?' Tyler's voice broke through the lust-fog that was killing her usual sensibilities.

She jerked her head back and twisted round to see Tyler glaring at them, his eyes flicking between Jody and Christian. And just like that the birds were tweeting and the ear-splitting roar of the chainsaw reappeared, putting the final nail in the coffin of whatever moment they'd just shared.

Jordan appeared behind Tyler with Mel in his wake. 'Yeah, were you going to kiss? It looked like it. Have you changed your mind about the kissing booth?

71

Were you going to have a practice?' Jordan made kissy noises.

'Jordan, leave your mum alone.' Mel swatted the top of his head with a tea towel. 'How did it go with Mr Thompson?'

Jody wrenched her hand out of Christian's and sprung up. 'Yeah, all sorted. He's agreed. Christian's in love with what Mr Thompson produces. I think he's quite keen to get naked with the cheese.' *Out of all the things to say, why had she mentioned Christian naked?* She closed her eyes, but not so fast she didn't see a sparkle appear in Mel's eye.

'Oh, out of every single thing in the village he could get naked with, it's the *cheese* he's most keen on. Well, colour me surprised.'

Jody forced her eyes open and, out of the corner of her eye, caught a glimpse of Christian, who was about the same colour as the eye fillet steak on Mr Thompson's butcher's block.

'Right, well…' Jody patted her pockets to make sure she had everything she needed to make a quick escape. 'Boys, go get your stuff. Business is done for the day. Let's go home and I'll get dinner on.'

Tyler spun on his heel and marched into the café, but Jordan hung about.

'You know, Mum, if you two were in love, that would be okay with me.' Jordan gave her a heart-melting smile. 'We've had heaps more time to play games. It's been awesome.' His grin widened before he turned and followed his brother into the café.

Jody shook her head, as much to clear her mind as to signal that she thought her son needed his head read. 'Boys. Honestly. The things that go through their minds. So crazy.' She shrugged and waited for Christian to echo her sentiments. He didn't.

CHAPTER FIVE

Jody tipped her face towards the sun and basked in its heat as the happy hum of the fair they were attending washed over her. *Please let the weather be like this for our festival.* Jody crossed her fingers and said a prayer to the weather gods. *Please keep the rain away. Sunshine only.*

'Hey, Mum. Look at that! How cool is that? We should get that for the festival.'

She opened her eyes to see Jordan pointing at something in the distance. What, she couldn't be sure of, as the fair's crowds milled around it, momentarily blocking her view. *And please let ticket sales pick up.* She paused, unsure whether there were such things as gods of crowds who would listen to and answer her prayers, of which there'd been a few in the last couple of days. Mainly prayers to the gods of anti-attraction, asking that there'd be no more intense moments between her and Christian. Prayers that she'd stop finding his smile more magnetic with every passing hour spent together. That his old business-only manner would return, because it was far less appealing than the relaxed, easy-going manner he'd adopted since the altercation with the butcher. The Christian she was spending time with now was charming, amusing and able to hold an adult conversation. A refreshing change, since her usual conversations turned to poo jokes or a wrestling match after ten seconds.

'Mum, you're not paying attention.' Jordan tugged at her hand. 'We need one of those, Mum. Say yes? Please? Come on, Christian, make her say yes. Or you say yes.' Jordan gave Christian a hopeful nod. 'Then it'll be two to one and we'll win.'

The crowds cleared for a second and Jody could see what had Jordan in a flap. A traditional popcorn cart. Painted cherry red, with two antique-style wheels and the word 'Popcorn' printed on the front in gold script. It was perfect.

'No need to gang up on me, boys. I love it. And it won't take up too much room, will it, Christian?'

Christian stroked his jaw in thought. 'No, it shouldn't do. I had Mrs Harper put together a list of local volunteers, so there'll be no problem finding someone to man it.'

'No surprise there. Mr Thompson may not be a fan of fixing up the pool, but the rest of the town are. And putting Mrs Harper on the case was a stroke of brilliance. People can't say no to her. She won't let them.'

'Well, I figured that job would stop her from putting her nose into the other aspects of the festival organisation. Seems I was mostly right. Except she did it so quickly I've got to figure out another thing to keep her busy. I know we can buy bunting cheaply, but I was thinking I could get her to make it by hand? I have contacts who could provide me with affordable material. We could end up saving money and Mrs Harper would be well busy...'

Jody laughed at the glint in Christian's eyes. At the previous day's committee meeting Mrs Harper had started pushing for the festival to be turned into a night affair complete with a fireworks display, and when that was nixed she'd started talking about having the local schoolkids put on a series of plays for the crowd's entertainment. Thankfully, Jordan and Tyler had been there to give her a definitive no, reminding her less than politely that they were already being forced to take part in the finale, even though they were meant to be on holiday, and it was bad enough they were being made to dress up as rabbits, without being forced into doing one thing more that required memorising, practising or taking direction.

'I think it'd keep her occupied. Handmade bunting...' she mused. 'I knew there was a reason I hired you.'

'Right. So that's settled, we're hiring a popcorn cart. We'll easily make our money back on that and the rest will be pure profit.'

'You know what else would be awesome, Mum?' Tyler tugged at her other arm. 'A candyfloss machine.'

Jody rolled her eyes. 'You say awesome, I say awful for your teeth. And the last thing we need is a bunch of kids running round the Leap on a sugar high. Their parents would never forgive us.'

'But, Muuuuum…'

'No whinging. My decision is final.'

'Tyler has a point…' Christian shuffled his feet from side to side, his hands shoved in his pockets, his gaze firmly on the ground.

'What do you mean, Tyler has a point?' Jody placed her hands on her hips. Who did Christian think he was, interfering with her parental right to say 'no'? 'I don't want him eating candyfloss. That stuff is pure sugar.'

'But it's not about what Tyler wants. Or what you want. It's about the festival, and candyfloss is so… festive. Pink fluffy clouds on sticks floating around the main street, gripped by happy punters. And the smell.' Christian finally met her steely stare. 'Seriously, Jody, breathe in.'

Jody inhaled the air, just a little bit so as not to appear churlish. But it was enough for sweet caramel notes to invade her olfactory senses. She could almost feel the candyfloss dissolving on her tongue. The sugar crystallising around the edges of her lips after taking a massive bite.

'We would also get a discount for hiring both machines. And the margins on candyfloss are brilliant.'

Christian was so right, Jody wanted to stamp the ground. And why had she thought he was trying to assert some sort of parental responsibility? It wasn't like he was her boyfriend or anything.

Or maybe it's that a small part of you has considered what he'd be like in that role?

Ugh. Mutinous mind. There was no way she'd thought about Christian like that. Sure, he had a pleasing-enough – okay, downright gorgeous – face. And yes, now he'd retrieved that stick from his bum, she'd discovered a person she enjoyed being around. But that didn't make for a boyfriend. And she didn't do boyfriends anyway. Ever. The last guy who'd been boyfriend material had disappeared into thin air after making her believe she was someone special. Leaving her with a bundle of baby-making cells in her stomach, and her dreams dashed.

Guilt hit her right in the solar plexus. It wasn't the boys' fault she'd had a one-night stand that had resulted in their existence and the death of her dreams to go to art school, to backpack around Europe, to paint and sculpt to her heart's content. She'd chosen her future, and thinking 'what if' was a waste of time.

'Shall we test the product?' There was one way to make the guilt go away. She'd feed her feelings until they were smothered in sticky sugar. Not waiting for an answer, Jody strode through the crowds in a murmur of 'excuse mes' until she reached the candyfloss stall. 'Four, please.'

She handed over the money and watched as the sugar was spun into wafting, blush-coloured balls of teeth-rotting goodness. She'd have to make sure they all drank water after this.

She didn't have to turn around to know the boys were behind her. Their excitement at being allowed this particularly rare form of sugary treat was tangible. They were bouncing about so much she wouldn't have been surprised to see a rare earthquake reported in the next day's papers.

'There you go.' The vendor passed the candyflosses over, one by one as they were done, and Jody passed them back to the boys. 'And here's the last one.'

Jody turned to give it to Christian, but he was nowhere in sight. She scanned the crowds but there was no sign of him. Well, that was perfect, just great. What was she going to do with the fourth stick? The boys would probably beg her to let them share it, but that wasn't going to happen, and throwing it in the bin wasn't an option. That would be a waste of money and she didn't waste money. Perhaps she could onsell it?

'Here.'

Something cool and wet was pressed against her forearm. Jody looked down. Bottles of water. How had Christian known? 'Thank you.' She nodded her gratitude as she swapped the bottles of water for the stick of candyfloss. 'Are you a mind reader? How did you know I'd be searching those out next?'

Christian plucked out a bunch of spun sugar and popped it in his mouth. Silent for a moment as he let the sugar melt. 'Not a mind reader. Not psychic. You forget that it's part of my job. Or it was. My first job

79

in the events world was as a lackey. It was part of my job to think ahead, to ensure people had what they wanted before they even knew they wanted it.'

'Well, you must have been very good at your job.'

'I'd like to think I was. I wouldn't be where I am if I hadn't been.'

Something unreadable flitted across Christian's face. A subtle tightening of his facial features. A hint of a frown line between his brows. Even his relaxed demeanour changed. His stance becoming taller, as if waiting for a battle. What did he think she was going to do? Accuse him of lying? Why would she? His website had listed his accomplishments, and she'd heard of many of the events he'd been part of. There was no reason to doubt him, was there?

'You know, I never did ask... Why did you take this job? I mean...it's a bit below your usual big-city festival or stadium concert. And the pay's...well, terrible.'

Christian folded his arms across his chest. His lips mashed together. His shoulder lifted, up and down, in a one-sided shrug. 'I was meant to be taking a holiday. But I'm not one for doing nothing, so I figured a change of pace would be as good as a holiday. And it really is. This job's a breeze. I'm enjoying it. Even if some of the committee are a little hard to manage at times.'

'Well, I'm glad you took us on. There was no way I'd have been able to manage them while doing the organising. We'd have ended up with a festi-fail,' Jody joked, hoping to lighten the mood. Something was up with Christian, but now wasn't the time to go into it. Not when two young boys were no longer in sight. Her heart picked up as panic set in. Where could they have gone? And what were they thinking, taking off without telling her? They didn't know this town. Neither did she. They could have gone anywhere and it would take hours to find them. And who knew what might happen during that time?

Damn it, she shouldn't have been directing her attention to the man before her; she was meant to put every single bit of her attention on them. That was the promise she'd made to them the moment they'd been born, as she held their tiny hands in hers. How had one man so quickly ruined a decade of determination to be the best parent possible? She mentally kicked herself as she weaved her way through the crowds, ditching the candyfloss in the first bin she saw, her appetite wrecked by worry. When she found the boys, she was taking them in each hand and not letting them go until they got home.

'Where did they go?' she muttered to herself.

'If I were them, I'd be heading that way,' said a voice at her side. Christian. Why did he sound so calm? So sure of himself? While she was struggling to contain herself, to stop herself from screaming their names.

She followed his finger, pointed just to their right. Towering high above the crowds, lazily circling, was a Ferris wheel. A waft of wind brought with it the tinkle of a carousel's music.

Jody pushed through the crowds to find the boys standing side by side, their heads tipped back, watching the big wheel go round. 'Do not ever run away without telling me where you're going,' Jody growled. 'If you ever do it again you're grounded from anything fun for a full month. And you won't be allowed out of your room apart from to go to the toilet or have a bath for a whole week.'

The boys jumped and turned to face her, delight disappearing from their faces. Regret rolled through her. Fear had made her harsh. The boys had been told off before, but never quite like that. Her throat ached from the coarseness of her tone.

'We just wanted to see it up close, Mum.' Tyler's eyes swam with unshed tears.

'It's so cool. Can we have one at our festival? Please?' Jordan begged, his eyes darting between Jody and Christian. 'Can we, Christian?'

'Maybe.' Christian stepped up beside them. 'But we have to choose between that and the carousel, so I guess that means, in order to decide, we'll have to ride on both and then make up our minds. But you boys have got to do one thing first. Give your mum a hug and promise her you'll never run off like that again.'

The boys rushed into Jody's arms, whispering sorry into her ears, wrapping their gangly arms around her. She gave Christian a small smile of thanks, and then buried her head in Jordan and Tyler's shoulders. Was this what having a partner was like? Sharing the load of parenthood. Working with each other. Having each other's backs. Being a team.

But she had a team, she reminded herself. A team of three. And they played perfectly well together. Rubbed along nicely. And there was no need to introduce a fourth member at this late stage of the game.

Jordan pulled away. 'So, can we go on the Ferris wheel now, Mum? Pleeeeeease.'

Above the boys' heads, Christian was nodding enthusiastically. 'Come on. It could be fun. You don't have anything against fun, do you?'

'No. Of course not. And you're right, we'll need to try both in order to make the best decision. So, Jordan, you sit with me. Tyler, you go with Christian.'

'But Mum…' Tyler's hands flew to his hips. 'Jordan and I want to do it together. It would be an adventure.'

'Yeah, Mum. We don't need you to hold our hands. We're big boys.'

Jody's heart wrenched. The boys were growing up. So fast. She was becoming dispensable. It wouldn't be long before they grew up. Left. Her team of three reduced to one.

A warm arm draped over her shoulder. She glanced up to see Christian standing next to her. 'Don't leave me hanging, Jody. The boys aren't the only ones who want to ride on that wheel. Come on, let's go.' He nudged her with his hip. 'Besides, if you don't come with me I'll look like some sad loser who couldn't get a date to the fair. My poor ego's feeling bruised at the thought.'

'Fine.' Jody went to shrug Christian's arm off, but stopped herself. Not because she liked it there or anything, but because she didn't want to be seen to be churlish after he'd been so good to the boys.

Sure. The voice of sarcasm rang loud and clear. *His arm's still slung around your shoulder for the boys' benefit. Yeah, right.*

Christian angled his head towards the sun, closed his eyes, breathed in the fresh air, revelling in the way it smelt so clean. Renewing. His first day in Rabbits Leap had left him believing he'd made a great mistake. That he should have stayed in London and faced the music. But now? Getting out of town had been the best idea. His nerves, taut from the anger he'd directed at himself for making one stupid and potentially fatal mistake, had been soothed by the relaxed atmosphere of the village. People went at their own pace. They didn't demand, they asked. There was no huffing if they had to wait a minute more than expected, and when they got what they wanted they said thank you and smiled. Rush hour wasn't a source of stress, it was a source of amusement as a quiet trickle of cars made its way to The Bullion. The bar below his quarters filling with the sounds of happy punters. He'd yet to brave the villagers, all too aware he didn't fit in with his designer clothes and expensive haircut. But maybe one day he would. Perhaps he could meet Jody there. Not in a date way, but in a friend way. Two people getting to know each other over a beer. Which sounded exactly like a date. And a nice one at that. Damn it.

'What's wrong?'

He opened his eyes to see Jody staring at him. Wrinkles of concern marring her smooth forehead.

'You looked peaceful for a second there. Happy. Then it was like a cloud came over your face.'

He gazed out over the milling crowds. Spotted a man and woman walking hand in hand. So close their shoulders were touching. Both laughing at a shared joke. What would it be like to have that?

'I was happy. It's pleasant up here. So peaceful.'

'Different to your usual life, then?' Jody unscrewed her water bottle and took a sip.

'Very.'

'Are you missing London? I know it's only been a few days but Rabbits Leap must be quite the culture shock.'

'It's certainly different. I've never seen so many dirty Wellingtons lined up outside a bar in my life. Hell, I've never seen Wellingtons lined up outside a bar full stop. But I'm enjoying it. I think this change of pace might actually be good for me.'

'Well, I'm glad to have given it to you. And thank you for making me go on this wheel. It's been... What's that word you used? Peaceful. You don't get a lot of peace with two boys around.' Her blue eyes darkened. She shook her head a little. 'Not that I don't want them to be them. I can't imagine life without those two ratbags of mine.'

'They strike me as good kids. Smart. Resourceful. Determined. I'd put that down to an exemplary upbringing.'

A small smile lit up Jody's face. 'Thanks. I've tried my best.'

'And your best is all you can do.' The words rang hollow in Christian's ears. In his family, 'your best' wasn't good enough. You had to push harder. Go further. And he had. So much so he was on the verge of losing everything.

The ground meandered towards them and it was time for the ride to end. They got off and made their way to the boys, who were waiting impatiently to the side.

'Christian, that was awesome! Did you love it? We loved it. We can't wait to go on one at our festival. It's going to be…'

'Don't tell me… It's going to be…awesome?'

'Yeah!' The boys jumped up and down, and held their hands up for high fives.

Their joy tugged at his heart, and he found himself high-fiving them and dancing a jig, while Jody laughed a metre away.

What was happening to him? From tough and disciplined order-barker to high-fiving jigger? Was Rabbits Leap changing him? Was it the boys and their enthusiastic ways? Or was it their mother? She didn't have any expectations of him. And without the fear of failure he was able to do his work in an easy-going, yet still efficient manner. He liked the effect her presence had on him. Hell, more than that, he liked *her*. A lot. More and more with every passing second. And in a way that was beyond friends.

'So, does this mean we've made up our minds?' Christian squatted down to the boys' level. The last thing he wanted or needed was for Jody to see any hint of desire in his face. He had the feeling it would scare her off, and he wanted to keep her close.

'Ferris wheel for the win!' Tyler held his hand up for another high five. 'We were up so high we could see the sea!'

Jody shook her head, her eyebrows raised in amusement. 'We could *almost* see the sea. But not quite. Not quite by a bit.'

'Sooooo…' Christian's ears pricked up at Jordan's wheedling tone. 'If Mum says yes, and if Tyler and I say yes, according to the deal…'

'But what about the carousel?' Christian teased, already knowing the answer. He waved his hand in dismissal. 'No, let's not bother with the carousel. Ferris wheel it is.'

'Awesome!'

'Freaking awesome!' The boys fist-bumped.

'Well, that's new,' Jody observed, drily. 'Where'd you learn that from?'

'One of Uncle Tony's movies. It's what the two main characters do when something cool happens,' Tyler explained. 'Mum, I'm hungry.'

'For a change.' Jody rolled her eyes.

'Well, I guess we could check out those food trucks?' Christian glanced up at Jody. 'See if we can convince your mum they're better than a bake sale...'

He was treated to an eye-roll of his very own. Followed by a curt nod. And a grin.

A grin from a mouth that, against his better judgement, he wanted to kiss.

CHAPTER SIX

Christian rapped on the folding table and its sharp echo bounced about the hall, snapping Jody out of her daze. Or her haze. Her hazy daze. The one she'd been in since she'd dropped Christian off at The Bullion after the fair. The outing had gone well. Too well.

She couldn't shake the image of Jordan and Tyler holding Christian's hands as they walked back towards the car. Their heads tilted towards him, their admiration obvious. Had insisting they come along to every festival recce been a bad idea? She could see that the more time they spent with him, the closer they got. How would they feel when he left? What would the impact be? The last thing she wanted the boys to feel was rejected. She'd worked too hard to ensure they had the love she'd barely experienced to let a man flit in and out of their lives, leaving a trail of tears behind him.

Jody covered her face with her hands and peered through a crack at Christian, whose eyebrows were arrowed together as he stared at his tablet, creating an inch-long crevasse between his brows. What was causing that frown? And why did she want to stroke that line away with her thumb, or kiss it?

Was seeing a man so comfortable with her boys causing her to soften her no-man stance? Or was it seeing the boys so comfortable? The way they'd gone on about Christian to her, you'd think they had as big a crush as she…

What? Noooooo. Oh no. Nope. She pushed her fingers tight together, erasing Christian from her sight. She did not have a crush on Christian. That would be crazy. She barely knew him. That wasn't how love worked.

What? Hold on. Hold up! Love? No. It was too soon for anything like that. Waaaaay too soon. All that was going on here was attraction, a little bit of like. Love was something that took time to build. Lots of time. And she'd known Christian all of a few days.

But they'd spent most of those few days together, which, if it was being measured in date time, would mean they'd been on about seven. Or eight. And from what she'd seen on television and movies, and read in magazines, date three was when something usually happened. And nothing had happened. So nothing was going to happen. There. Sorted. Nothing to worry about.

'Jody? Are you okay over there? Is the light getting in your eyes? Shall I draw the blinds?'

Jody pressed her hands closer to her mouth, smothering a groan. And why did he have to be so thoughtful? On top of good to look at? She needed more hands. One lot to cover her eyes. Another lot to cover her ears. One last lot to push Christian away.

'Are you sick, Jody?' asked Mrs Harper, who was sitting to her left. 'Morning sickness?'

This time Jody didn't bother to stifle the groan.

'Oh, Shirley. You know better than that. Our Jody doesn't have anything to do with men. Morning sickness is not an option, more's the pity. She makes such lovely children. And oh, how the village could do with another baby to snuggle. Lord knows Serena is never having kids at this rate. Hasn't even looked at a man since she returned home.'

'Well, rules are made to be broken, and there's a first time for everything. And you know it's not like we've had fresh blood in the village any time lately... Well, until now.'

Jody slid her hands from her face in time to see Mrs Harper's knowing look darting between herself and Christian.

A cough-choke filled the room.

'Need some water, Christian?' Mrs Harper asked, innocently.

'I'm fine. Really. Just need to get a move on with this meeting, all right?' He cleared his throat again and prodded at his tablet's screen. 'Mrs Harper, how's the bunting creation going?'

'Great, although why I have to make it from scratch I don't know. Surely buying it is a better option?'

'Well it would be an easier option, but I was able to secure a good deal on fabric, making it cheaper than buying it. And since the goal is to keep the budget down, and you're willing to make it for free, it was the best option.'

'I see your point. Doesn't mean I like it,' Mrs Harper grumbled, her nose screwed up in distaste. 'I'm on top of it. Also on top of promotion. My son's shown me my way around the interwebs and social media. Quite frankly I wish he had sooner. You won't believe the people I'm connecting with. That's what they call it, you know? Connecting. The stories they have to tell.' She leaned in conspiratorially. 'I heard the florist three towns over...'

'Mrs Harper, we don't need to know anything about the florist three towns over. What we need to know is that you're getting the message out there.'

Mrs Harper leant back in her chair, arms folded, her nose clearly out of joint. 'Have ticket sales picked up?'

'Yes.'

'Well then, I'm doing my job.'

'Great. Good work.' Christian squinted at his screen, completely missing Mrs Harper's tongue-poke. 'So, we've organised three food trucks. Jody has convinced me the bake sale should still happen. Apparently if we have savoury, we need to have sweet.'

'Hear, hear!' clapped Mrs Hunter.

'We're hiring on top of that a popcorn and candyfloss machine, and we're all sorted for kids entertainment... I just need to check out the ponies we're hiring to ensure they'll be safe with the little ones. What else could we bring to the table? Something a little different. Something to pique people's interest…'

'What about a psychic!?' Mrs Harper motioned to something just outside the hall's door. 'How fun would that be?'

'As in one of those booths where you put money in and some creepy-looking doll tells you your fortune? I'm sure we could find space for that. Maybe somewhere out of the way. We could decorate it to look a little eerie…'

'No. I mean a real one. Ms Millie.'

'Ooooh, Ms Millie!' Mrs Hunter's greying curls bobbed furiously in agreement. 'She's the one who predicted my Serena would come back home, and that she'd find her destiny here. She's never wrong.'

'And she's told me my boys will one day give me grandchildren. She's not yet right, but I have faith.' Mrs Harper gave a curt nod. 'And she's keen. In fact she's waiting outside. I thought you'd like to meet her, Christian. Ms Millie said you might have some issues she'd need to talk to you about.'

Christian picked up his tablet and stood up. 'No, no need to chat to Ms Millie. I have no issues, other than we can't afford her and couldn't find the space for a setup like that. Meeting adjourned.'

Jody sat up straighter in her chair. Was it her imagination or did Christian look…rattled? Was he nervous about meeting Ms Millie? Why? She was harmless. She did have a spooky way of predicting the future according to those who went to visit her, but

93

from what Jody had heard, Ms Millie never predicted anything harmful. So why was Christian stalking to the door like he had a pack of feral dogs at his heels?

'Oh, there you are!' a throaty voice boomed, as a shadow darkened the hall's entranceway. 'I've been longing to meet you. Christian, isn't it?'

Christian stopped. Took two steps backwards. Even from half a hall away, Jody could see his neck muscles bunched tight, his shoulders rising. His hand gripped his tablet so hard his knuckles bulged a purply white.

Ms Millie swept into the hall in a flourish of pink and green silk caftan. Her bright-orange hair piled high on her head, on top of which a fake parrot resided. 'It's truly a pleasure to meet you.' She thrust her hands out and caught Christian's free hand, pumping it vigorously. 'So, I hear you want me to have a stall at your little festival. No. Hold on. I'm wrong.' She angled her head, her eyes searching the hall's ceiling as if looking for an answer. 'The *big* little festival. That's right, isn't it?'

Christian nodded. His face had gone ashen, Jody noted, and perspiration peppered his temples. Was he really that scared?

'So, I hear I'm going to be a star attraction?' Ms Millie batted her eyes at Christian. 'There'll be a tent, of course, covered in rugs, with gauze draped from the ceiling. And cushions for myself, the customers and my pet poodle, Fifi, to sit on.'

'Um, is this a prediction? Have you seen this?' Christian asked, taking a sidestep, then another, around Ms Millie, who copied his actions, resulting in them appearing to be doing some sort of complicated dance.

'Not a prediction, dear. Just an order. I'm happy to give my time for free for this marvellous event. How could I not? I can't wait to be able to slip into my bikini and do a few laps in the pool. I can see you'll be joining me...'

Christian's eyes bulged. Jody smothered a laugh.

'And *that*, my dear, isn't an order. That's a prediction.'

Christian shook his head and attempted another two sidesteps. His escape was thwarted by the appearance of Fifi, blocking the door, yapping madly.

'There's my girl! My poopsie darling! Good girl. You keep this fine specimen from escaping while I tell him his future. I can see he'll need some convincing.'

Ms Millie lunged for his hand and jerked it towards her, turning it palm-side up. 'Let me see...' She peered down intently. 'Hmmm...'

'What...what...what does "hmmm" mean?' Christian choked out, his face now no longer ashen but a worrying shade of green.

Jody stood up and made to stand beside him, to give him some support should he need it, but Ms Millie waved her away. 'No, you go over there. I can't have you interfering with this. You're too closely linked.'

Too closely linked? What was Ms Millie on about? They worked together, sure. But that hardly made them linked in any way. And yes, there was that hum of something between them. But that was just hormones, or chemicals, or something. Nothing serious. Nothing *linked*. Unless she meant they would be linked in *that* way. As a man and woman were wont to be…

Jody backed away and plopped back down in her chair. No? Surely not? Really? Her cheeks heated up as if she'd stepped under one of the warming lamps in Tony's kitchen. The idea wasn't horrible. Quite the opposite. But it had been so long… And she had made that vow…

One night of pleasure doesn't mean you've broken the vow. One and done. It's doable. As doable as Christian is.

Her cheeks reached inferno level. Thank God Mrs Harper and Mrs Hunter were too busy focusing on whatever was going on between Christian and Ms Millie, otherwise they'd be giving her quite the interrogation.

Could she do it? Should she? Would she even remember what to do? She recalled how right her hand had felt tucked in Christian's. How every time they'd touched, no matter how inadvertently, it had felt natural. Right. And even if she were rusty, she had no doubt Christian would be able to take control. To reawaken the passion that had slumbered for so long.

The heat in her cheeks erupted, spilling down through her body, heading straight to her core. She wanted him. All of him. Damn it. She wanted to wrap her arms around his neck and to pull his lips down to hers…to see if they were as soft, yet demanding, as they appeared. To discover if he tasted of that citrus scent she'd been trying not to inhale since the moment they'd met. Her need for him was hypnotic. Like a tractor beam, her boys would say.

Her boys.

And just like that an icy-cold bucket of water was thrown on her lust.

They were what mattered. Not her. Not the man standing a few metres away from her.

'I see some sort of trouble following you. You can't outrun it. I don't know that you could if you tried…'

Ms Millie's words further pulled Jody out of her fantasy. What trouble? What was she going on about, and why was Christian in a tug of war with Ms Millie? Yanking his hand away from her, while she was pulling it straight back.

'But you need to face up to things more. You must. Then you can have the future you deserve. The future that's written in the stars. And what a big little future it will be.'

'That. Is. Enough.' Each word punctuated with another tug, each stronger than the one before, until Christian was able to rip his hand free. His face pink with exertion, his chest rising and falling. 'I've heard enough of this tripe.'

Ms Millie smiled, apparently unrattled at having her talents called tripe. 'You know I see the truth. You just have to believe in yourself. And trust in the process. Also, relax. Seriously. Being uptight's not going to get you anywhere. Now, go and have lunch with Jody. It will do you good.' She glanced over at Jody, a sly smile on her face. 'It will do you *both* good.'

'That's the one sentence you've said that makes any sense. Jody, we could talk about the musical entertainment over a meal?' Christian turned to her and crooked his arm.

There was no way she was touching him, sliding her arm through his. Not after she'd all but succumbed to him minutes before…in her mind anyway.

'Lunch sounds great.' She picked up her bag and made her way towards the door, ignoring the way Christian's face fell at her brush-off. 'We'll pick the boys up at the park and bring them with us. They'll be famished.'

If the boys were there, she'd be safe from her thoughts. Her desires. The boys would keep her in line, just as they always had.

CHAPTER SEVEN

'It must be hard watching them grow up.' Christian nodded to the boys who'd seated themselves at another table at the opposite end of the pub, telling Jody they wanted to give her some adult time. The boys had turned their backs on her as soon as they'd issued their decision, so hadn't seen Jody's face fall. But he had. And his heart had gone out to her. She lived for her boys, that much was obvious. But did that leave Jody any time for herself? From the way Mrs Hunter had been talking, she wasn't seeing anyone. Or was even interested in doing so.

Jody cupped her chin in her hand. 'Yeah,' she sighed. 'It's hard. I feel like every day I wake up to them being less like boys and more like young men. They're not my babies any more, even though I tell them, much to their disgust, that they'll always be my babies.' She drummed her fingers on her cheek. Christian sensed a change of topic was afoot. 'So, tell me, what happened back there in the hall? You seemed...kind of freaked out. And what was all that talk about trouble?'

Apparently his attempt to appear stoic and unruffled during the reading had failed. Christian picked up the menu and pretended to focus on the food descriptions. Not that he saw any of them. He was still shaken, and feeling a little sick with it too. He'd always believed fortune telling was a load of codswallop. Something people did to fleece poor, unsuspecting souls out of money in exchange for hope.

As soon as Ms Millie had been mentioned, he knew he didn't want to meet her because, despite his lack of belief, there was still that element of 'what if' involved. And despite his rational mind reassuring him she'd be a fake, she'd said things to prove him wrong.

Ms Millie had seen the stupid mistake he'd made that, once discovered, would lead to his downfall. Once people knew what he'd done, he'd be well and truly out of work. And without work what else did he have? Nothing. He didn't work to live, he lived to work. It was all he knew. And he didn't know whether he could unlearn that attitude. A week in Rabbits Leap was doing wonders for his stress levels, but surely he'd soon miss the hustle, the vibrancy, the breakneck pace of the city.

'Christian?' Jody prompted. 'Don't tell me she actually predicted something?'

'What? No.' Christian set his menu down. 'I have no idea what she was talking about. I just didn't appreciate being set upon by a woman wearing a fake bird on top of her head. It was very disconcerting.'

Jody giggled. 'She has a whole flock of them, you know? Changes daily. She's a character. And, I hate

100

to say it, and I know you won't like it, but I think she'd be good fun for the festival. Also, it'd keep both Mrs Hs off our back if they felt like they got their way on something.'

Christian picked up his menu again. Now they were on work territory again his appetite had returned. 'So, is anything taking your fancy?'

Jody's eyes met his over the menus, locked. A flicker of something that looked a lot like hunger, but not of the food-related kind, appeared. A beautiful flush coloured Jody's cheeks. Her eyes brightened, sparkled.

'The scallops. What about you? See anything you're interested in?'

Christian nodded. Jody might not be in the market for a boyfriend, but that didn't mean she wasn't interested. And if he were reading things correctly, the attraction he felt was officially mutual. 'Yes. In fact there is.'

'You right, sis?' Tony appeared with a notebook in one hand, a pen in the other, ready to take their order. 'You look flustered. Need some water? Something stronger?'

'Perhaps she needs a lie-down?' Christian replied smoothly. 'She's been working very hard. Going to bed would be an excellent idea.'

Jody clasped the glass of water and downed it. 'No, I'm fine. No bed. Not ever. Well, not until later. By myself. Tony, I want the scallops.'

'Are you sure you're okay?' There was no missing the twinkle in Tony's eye.

'I'm *fine*, Tony. Now do your job and ask Christian what he'd like to eat.'

Tony turned his attention to Christian. 'And what can I get you? Feel free to say my sister, because I love seeing her eyes bug out of her head in irritation.'

Christian set his menu down with a smile and focused his attention on Jody. 'Your sister.'

Jody picked up her water glass and aimed its contents in Christian's direction, and then Tony's. 'There's enough water in this glass to soak one of you, and right now I'm not sure who deserves it the most.'

'Woah, calm down, Jodes.' Tony took a step away. 'We're just teasing.'

'And I'm working on three hours sleep. This festival business is keeping me awake all hours, so my tolerance is even less than usual. So, Christian, answer the question. Tony, take the order. And let's get this lunch done. I've washing to fold and a kitchen floor to mop, and I need to finish the design for the kids' rabbit costumes and get them off to the Stitch 'n' Snitch club.' Jody set her glass down with a clunk. 'They've got their work cut out for them if they're to get it all done in time. They might not even have time to gossip.'

'I don't suppose Mrs Harper's part of that club?' Christian grinned.

Jody giggled. 'She's the head of it.'

'Surprise, surprise. This town of yours never fails to amuse me.' Christian turned to Tony. 'And I'll have the steak with blue cheese sauce.'

Tony wrote the order down with a nod. 'Any drinks?'

'Some wine perhaps? A bottle of pinot gris?' Christian looked to Jody for her agreement.

She shook her head. 'No. I don't want to work on a fuzzy head. I'll stick with water.'

'You don't want to drink because of work? That's not the sister I know and love.' Tony raised his eyebrows. 'Perhaps you're afraid a little wine will bring down those inhibitions of yours. Make you break your own rules...'

Jody's nostrils flared in irritation. 'Tony, you've customers. Go do your job.'

Tony left with a wink and a laugh.

Jody relaxed back into her chair. 'God, that brother of mine does not know when to stop. Just pushes and pushes an issue and then gives it one more nudge.'

'What is it with this rule I keep hearing about? No men? Are people joking?'

'Why would they joke?' Jody focused on her water glass as she slowly spun it round.

Christian searched her face. It was straight, no hint of teasing. 'Well, it's just...you're an intelligent, funny and good-looking woman. And you're single. Apparently. And it appears you don't even date. Why is that?'

Jody's head angled to the left. Towards the boys. 'I don't have time to date. I'm raising boys. I have my farm to run. Small as it is, it still takes up a lot of time, even with Jack on hand doing most of the work. When I'm not working on accounts or looking after the boys, I like to work on my art. I don't have time to pander to the wants and needs of another human.'

Why did something in that statement not ring quite true? 'Perhaps. Although I've seen you give so much to this community in the short time I've been here. I suspect you don't mind pandering to other people. Is it something to do with the boys' father? Did he break your heart?'

Jody forced herself to keep a straight face, to not let any hint of the annoyance she felt whenever she thought of the boys' dad show. Christian didn't need to know how one night had changed her destiny. More than that, it had changed her world view. And solidified her view of herself. There was only one thing for it. She'd have to tell a white lie. 'You can't have your heart broken by a man you only knew for one night.'

Christian's forehead crinkled in surprise. Jody smiled to herself. Game, set and end-match to her.

'So it was a…'

'One-night stand.'

He picked up his fork, set it down again. She'd rattled him. Good.

'But, how?'

Jody couldn't stop herself from smirking. 'Christian, you're a grown man. I'm sure you understand how a one-night stand works.'

'Well, yes.' Christian stroked his chin, his eyes narrowing in thought. 'But I guess…'

'You can't imagine a lady such as I partaking in such a scandalous act?'

'Well…yes.'

'Let me paint a picture. Young Jody worked in this very bar. Young Jody met a guy who wasn't from around these parts. Young Jody drank tequila. Young Jody fell into bed with said guy. Two months later Young Jody discovered the guy had given her more than just a raging hangover, he'd given her two babies. Condom. Fail.'

'Oh. Ooooooh... Oh.' Christian raked his hand through his hair, then repeated the action. He was cute when he was flustered. 'So, do the boys have anything to do with him?'

'He has no idea they exist.' Jody kept her tone even. Didn't let the ache in her heart that more members of her family would grow up with only one parent show. Still, at least she cared for her sons, loved them to the ends of the ever-expanding universe and back, and made sure she showed it, unlike her father, who'd barely acknowledged the presence of his children after their mother passed away.

'Isn't that...wrong...to deny them a chance to know their father?'

The blood in Jody's veins pulsed with hot indignation. Did he really assume she hadn't tried to find the boys' dad? 'Christian, how easy do you think it is to find a blond-haired, blue-eyed Australian named "Dan" who likes to surf and travels the world doing so.'

Christian's hitched-up shoulders deflated. 'Not easy, I imagine.'

'I still search social media sites every now and then, just in case. But I'd have a better chance of finding the world's smallest needle in the world's largest haystack.'

'So there's no chance of him returning to Rabbits Leap?'

Jody cough-laughed. Harsh, guttural. 'He only ended up here by accident. Was heading to the coast to catch some waves, took a wrong turn. Got lost in the dark and decided to crash the night here. He's not coming back. There's no reason to. As far as he's aware, anyway.'

'So he got to continue his life, catching waves, doing his own thing. And you got to raise two boys and put your dreams on hold... So did you plan to stay here? Before the boys came along?'

How did he do that, Jody wondered. How could he read her so well? 'Are you asking me if I'm a homey person by design or fate?'

'I'm just asking...'

'I think you know the answer.' Jody glanced around the pub, taking in the locals and out-of-towners who had gathered for lunch, laughing, smiling, happy in their lives. Was she? She batted the thought away as guilt set in. There was no point in being anything but happy with her life. She'd made her choice, she'd had her boys, and now it was her job to be the best mother she could. To create the best family she could.

'So you would have done something else? Gone somewhere else? Had motherhood not come calling?' Christian fixed her with a shrewd eye, causing the guilt that had settled in the pit of her stomach to bloom. 'Did you have dreams of doing more with your life?'

Jody picked up her glass, took a sip of the water, and silently wished the food would hurry up so she could scoff it back and get away from this man with his intense eyes and almost psychic methods of interrogation. Perhaps he should have his own booth, instead of Ms Millie. Jody bit the inside of her cheek and forced herself to relax. 'Don't most eighteen-year-olds?' She plastered an easy smile on her face. 'I always wanted to travel through Europe, see great works of art. But it's no big deal that it hasn't happened yet. I have all the time in the world to make those dreams come true. As you observed, the boys are growing up. Once they're out in the world living their dreams, I'll live mine.'

'Indeed.' Christian half-shrugged.

'So what was your dream growing up, Christian?' Jody sat back in her seat and glared at her brother, who had a knowing smirk on his face as he placed their meals down before beating a hasty retreat.

'My dream?' Christian picked up his cloth napkin, shook it out and placed it on his lap. A little vein pulsed at his temple, his jaw twitched. What about that question had made him so tense? 'Well, I wanted to be a superhero. To save people. But when I grew up and realised that wasn't a job, I decided, if I couldn't be a superhero, I'd be the most super, in-demand event manager in London. I might not have been saving people's lives, but I was saving their lives from being boring by creating the best events.'

'And obviously you've done that. Your credentials are very impressive.'

A shadow crossed Christian's face. Jody looked out of the window to see if a cloud had covered the sun. But no. There were no clouds, just brilliant sunshine spilling into the restaurant.

'I can be better. I can be, I *will* be, the best of the best.' He eyed his steak with distaste. It looked fine to Jody, better than fine. Had something she'd said made Christian lose his appetite?

Jody speared a plump scallop and ran it over the drizzle of basil pesto. 'When will you know that you're the "best of the best"? And will you move on to something else once you've reached this lofty goal of yours?'

'If I'm honest with you, Jody, I don't know I could stop, even if I became the best in the world, even if I hit retirement age. Event management is in my heart, my soul. It's what I love to do. And in all honesty it's what gives me a reason to live. To stop working would leave me with nothing.'

Jody paused, shocked at Christian's honesty. 'Surely that's not true. You must have friends and family back in London. A girlfriend?' She held her breath, hating the way the answer to that question mattered to her.

'Friends, yes. But they're as busy as I am, so catch-ups are rare. Family is a mother and a father. Both incredibly successful in their fields. We don't see each other often. They don't care for my choice of career.'

'Which is why you strive to be the best? To prove them wrong?'

'Something like that.' Christian prodded the steak with his fork. 'And no girlfriend. I mean, I have had girlfriends. But they don't tend to work out. They get sick of taking a backseat to my work. I'm always honest and upfront with them. Always explain that work comes first. That I'm not the flowers and chocolates and walks on the beach type of guy, but that I'll support them if they support me.'

'Sounds like a business arrangement to me.' Jody tried to ignore her disappointment. Christian's views on relationships were a good thing. They'd keep her safe. Stop her from falling for the wrong man. From trusting the wrong man. Again.

Christian nodded. 'I guess it is. It worked for my parents. They're still together.' The words came out constricted. Tight with unshed emotion. The tautness in his jaw told her something was wrong, but it wasn't up for discussion.

'Well, maybe you're all on to something, because experience has taught me that not a lot of good comes from that dreamy, romantic kind of passionate love.' She sucked in the side of her cheek and clenched on the soft flesh. Damn it. She'd said too much.

'So the boys' father did hurt you?'

Jody released her cheek. Perhaps if she put the truth out there this attraction she felt between herself and Christian would be extinguished. He'd see she wasn't worth sticking around for. Not that that was on the cards, nor did the rational side of her want it to be. 'Yeah, well, I was stupid. Things weren't great at home when Dan walked into the bar. We stayed up all night talking about our plans, what we wanted to do with our lives, where we wanted to go, and I don't know… somewhere along the way I got the feeling he was happy for me to join him on his travels. We'd be great adventurers, travelling the world. Him surfing. Me painting. I'd sell my paintings to fund further travel. I let myself believe it was soulmate talk, not what it actually was, which was drunk talk. I woke up. He was gone. No note in sight.' The words came out mechanically. They had to. Any emotion injected into them would see tears falling. And her scallops didn't need extra salt. 'Anyway, enough about me. Let's talk about work.'

'But…' Christian interrupted.

'No. No buts. That's as much as you're getting out of me.' She leaned over and fished her phone out of her bag. 'You mentioned there were a couple of musical acts we could check out? When and where?'

Christian dabbed at his lips with the serviette and pushed the plate away. 'You're not going to like what I have to say.'

Jody's stomach went into free-fall. Had all the good bands been booked already? Was this the beginning of a festival flop? 'What do you mean? Don't tell me the only bands available are death metal or some pan flute one-man-band?'

'No. I've found a good jazz band, and a rock 'n' roll band. The rock 'n' roll band's playing tonight at a bar in Exmouth, and the jazz band's got a gig the next day in Tiverton, which I thought we could catch on the way back.'

'So, what are you saying?' Jody's stomach did a swandive. She knew what was coming next.

'I'm saying I think it would be a good idea to stay overnight in Exmouth, and make a proper trip of it.' Christian looked around the room, saw Tony and waved him over.

'But who'd look after the boys while we were away? Remember what I said? There's no one to look after them. It's just me.' Jody watched as Tony threaded his way between the tables. He was looking pleased with himself. Too pleased. Something was up.

He reached their table with an extra spring in his step. 'I hear you need a babysitter so you can have a night off from the ratbags.'

'Oh really? You've heard that, have you? I wonder who from?' She turned to Christian and shot him a murderous look.

'I have. And I'm here to offer my services. Actually, I'm offering my services, Mel's services, and Mel's mum's services. Between the three of us we can take care of them. Mel's mum will take care of them this afternoon at the café. They'll come home with Mel and, since it's her night off, she'll be upstairs, which means they'll have a watchful ear on them. Then I can hang out with them here tomorrow until you get back. And the farm is safe in Jack's hands. Sorted, see?' Tony gave her an encouraging nod. 'Go on, Jodes. Give yourself a break. It's only been nearly ten years since you had one. You deserve it.'

Jody gave Tony a withering glance. 'Well, doesn't this sound like a fait accompli?'

'Or a perfect plan,' Christian added. 'I want your approval of the bands. You'll know better than I do if the people from around these parts will enjoy them. Also, I'm tone deaf, so if these bands are actually terrible, I wouldn't know.'

'You're tone deaf? How does that work? I'd have thought an event manager would need a perfect pair of ears.'

'Back in London I have a team of people who support me. I couldn't do the events I do without them. But I couldn't afford to bring them here, obviously. Which is why you're to come with me. You're my team.'

'And where will we be staying?' Jody asked, attempting to throw up barriers. 'It's summer. Exmouth will be heaving with people. I very much doubt there's any accommodation available at such short notice.'

'I have a friend who has a place there. He's not using it at the moment. We're more than welcome to stay.'

'It's got two bedrooms?' The swooping in Jody's stomach picked up pace. 'I'm not sleeping in the same bed as you. Sorry.'

'Yeah, you sound it. And yes, two bedrooms. We'll have to share a bathroom, though. Can you handle that?'

Tony snorted. 'I like this guy, Jodes. He's got a sense of humour. And he's got you right where he wants you.

Just say yes, and stop making excuses. Go see a band. Dance – by yourself if you can't bear to let a man hold your hands or wrap an arm around your waist. Sleep in. Have a leisurely breakfast.'

'Stop making this sound like it's a good idea, Tony,' Jody growled.

'I'm just calling it like I see it.'

Jody mashed her lips together. She was stuck. Saying no wasn't an option, because technically it was her job to organise the festival. But saying yes felt like it wasn't going to lead anywhere good. The last time she'd been in a bar with a man she'd found attractive, she'd wound up becoming a mother.

'I'm taking your silence as a "yes". Thanks, Tony. We'll leave at three this afternoon.' Christian flicked Tony the thumbs-up.

'Have fun, Christian. And Jodes? Make sure you don't take those daggers with you.'

'Daggers?' grunted Jody.

'The ones coming out of your eyes right now.' Tony laughed, and left them to check on another table.

'I can't believe you colluded against me with my brother.' Jody grabbed her bag and stood up. 'For that you can pay for lunch. And don't expect me to say a word to you the whole entire time we're away. You're in my bad books, buddy.'

Christian fished his wallet out of his pocket. 'At least I'm in your books. From what I can tell, I'm the first man to even be on your radar in a very long time. I count myself privileged.'

'You're infuriating.' She turned on her heel and strode out of the pub, but not fast enough to miss Christian's final words.

'And you're beautiful when you're angry. And when you're not.'

Ugh. It was only twenty-four hours. She could resist her attraction to Christian for one day. Surely she could?

But that swan swooping about in her stomach told her otherwise.

CHAPTER EIGHT

Christian tried to focus on the narrow road ahead of him. But his attention kept wandering to the woman sitting statue-still next to him. She was definitely making good on her promise not to say a word to him. Jody baffled him. Their attraction to each other was obvious, yet, despite a few moments when she'd let her shield down, she resisted it with every fibre of her being. To an extent he understood. He'd never, not once, got involved with a woman who wanted a traditional relationship. The whole happy families thing felt like the ultimate time-suck. Why waste time reading stories in bed when you could be making a name for yourself. Or trying to prove to disapproving people that their way wasn't the only way. That success was success, even if it didn't mean wearing scrubs or robes. But since he'd begun to get to know Jody and the boys, seen what love and affection looked like, he'd found his determination to stay family-free to be...sad.

He'd always prided himself on his independence, but now it felt less independent and more lonely, and in the last couple of days he'd found himself reassessing his stance. Surely, if he could, Jody could too? And they didn't have to be happily ever after. Not if Jody didn't want to. But surely she needed to let off steam? Needed to have fun? And one night or two of adult fun never hurt anyone. As long as they both knew the score...

'Jody, I can't believe you're actually serious about not dating until the boys have grown up.'

He waited for an answer, but was unsurprised when none was forthcoming.

'I can see you've made them your life. I get that. They're your biggest responsibility. But surely that attitude of yours can't be healthy, for you I mean. Before you were a mum you were a budding artist. And I always thought an artist needed inspiration and passion in their life...' Out of the corner of his eye he saw her mouth part ever so slightly, then shut. Her front teeth sinking into her lower lip. She didn't glance his way. Her full focus remained on the passing fields, lush and green, and the stunning meadows, filled with brilliantly coloured wildflowers.

A mild breeze blew in as Jody pushed down on the electric button for her window. She closed her eyes and inhaled the fresh country air, giving Christian a moment to appreciate the woman beside him. He'd said she was beautiful back at the pub, and while it had been in good humour, it wasn't said in jest. She really was beautiful. Her curly hair danced on her shoulders, serving to emphasise the delicate lines of her collarbone. Her lips were lush and full, yet soft. Kissable. Her cheekbones high. And little lines of laughter were only beginning to etch themselves around her eyes. What would it be like to run his hands over those lines? Over her curves? To feel her under him. On top of…

'Stop looking at me.'

Christian grinned and fixed his stare on the road ahead. 'I wasn't. And it's nice we're talking again.'

'We're not talking. I'm issuing an instruction. And it didn't feel to me like you weren't looking.' Jody opened one eye. 'Don't forget, I have two kids, I know when something's up. When mischief is in the making.'

'Is that so? Well, what mischief was in the making, pray tell?' Christian plastered an innocent expression on his face and glanced over at Jody.

He was rewarded with a blush, starting at her cheeks and spilling down her neck.

'You're not just a wonderful artist and excellent mother, Jody McArthur. It seems you're up there with Ms Millie in terms of sensing stuff about people. Anyway, it wouldn't matter what I was thinking, would it?' Christian turned on to the main road. 'You're the untouchable woman.'

Jody hit the button to wind her window up, then turned the air-con up, bringing a chill to the atmosphere. A subtle way of reminding him she would freeze out any advances? That she couldn't be thawed? Or was the 'I have no interest in men' somewhat of a front? Christian suspected so. A woman like Jody would never be truly cold. She was too warm and inviting. Beneath that 'I'm here for my boys only' exterior he'd bet was a woman who was just waiting to experience love, passion, desire. A woman who, once she'd found it, would come truly alive. Be the best version of herself. And the more time he spent with Jody, the more he wanted to be the man to release that in her. He wanted to hit her ignition, to see her fire up.

They turned on to the M5 and the journey carried on in silence. Christian prayed the bands would be okay, because if they weren't this whole trip was going to be a bust.

Farmland gradually faded, and the wonders of not-so-modern technology started to pervade. Traffic lights. Gangly streetlights towering above copious amounts of cars. Rows of houses with perfectly manicured lawns and gardens tucked away behind brick or stone walls. Businesses flogging accommodation, entertainment, food and beverages. And then they hit the waterfront.

'It's beautiful,' Jody breathed, as the sea twinkled and sparkled under the rays of the late-afternoon sun. 'I'd forgotten.'

'When's the last time you were here?' Christian asked cautiously, not wanting to say or do anything that would wipe away the every-bit-as-bright-as-the-sun smile that lit up Jody's face.

'Years ago. Back when Mum was alive. We'd come here for a holiday every year. Dad would even join us during the day before heading back to the pub in the afternoon. But Mum, Tony and I would stay for a whole week. Eating ice cream for breakfast. Spending all day building sandcastles. Swimming until we were shivering messes. Then warming ourselves under the sun, only to repeat the process over and over again until it was time for fish and chips for dinner. It's amazing we didn't get scurvy on those holidays. I don't think we ate a single healthy thing.'

'And you've never brought the boys here?'

Goosebumps rippled over Jody's skin. 'No. This probably sounds stupid, but I guess part of me wants to keep those memories as my own. I don't want any other experience to intrude on them. Selfish, huh?'

Christian checked his sat nav to see how close they were to the flat. 'So no memory-making while we're here?'

'That's right. Get in. Firm up the booking if we like what we see. Get out.'

'What about memory-making in Tiverton? Anything happen there that you don't want erasing or muddying-up?' he teased, enjoying the rosy glow of her cheeks. She might be annoyed with him, but that chemistry was still there. Taunting. Tempting...

'Can't say I've ever had any major events happen in Tiverton.' Jody tapped at her chin. 'Nope. Not one. Although booking the last band would be good. That would be the last thing sorted for the festival. Then you'll be free of us. Able to head home until the day itself.'

Was Christian imagining it, or did he detect a note of sadness? And was that disappointment making his heart feel like a brick had been placed upon it? Was he

119

going to be sad to leave Rabbits Leap? Surely not. 'No doubt you'll all be glad to see me and my interfering ways go.' Christian manoeuvred into a car park. His gaze flicked over to Jody to see her response. Her eyes were firmly trained on the car in front of them. Another brick was placed upon his heart. What was going on with him? 'Well, we're here.'

Jody craned her neck to look behind them. 'And we're only half a street away from the sea. Does that mean there's a chance we'll have a view?'

Christian winked, then got out of the car, opened the boot and grabbed their bags. He watched as Jody stepped into the bright sunshine, lifting her arms high over her head in a deep stretch. Jody was going to be delighted. And he was glad to be the person to delight her.

'Come on then. Follow me.' He started down the street and rounded the corner onto the waterfront. The quick slap of Jody's sandals told him she wasn't far behind. He stopped outside a lilac-coloured two-floor flat. Bright red and pink geraniums bloomed their welcome along the wrought-iron fence.

'This is it? This is where we're staying?' Jody turned to face him, then punched him on the arm. 'You rotter! You made it sound like we were staying in some sort of basic hovel!'

'I never did.' Christian rubbed his arm. 'I said it was a "place" and this is the place.'

'It's amazing! What's it like inside?' Jody grabbed his sleeve and pulled him through the gate and up to the door. 'Go on, open it.'

Christian looked about for the stone under which his friend had organised for his housekeeper to stow away the key. Spotting it, he fished it out and unlocked the door, opening it wide so Jody could rush in and explore to her heart's content.

Except she didn't.

'Well, go on. Don't just shift from foot to foot, awkwardly gnawing on that bottom lip of yours. Go look. It's yours for one night.'

'Come with me?' Jody held her hand out.

Christian took her hand in his and together they crossed the threshold. Their arms pressed together as they squeezed through the small door. Those increasingly familiar zaps of something more than friendship raced up and down the right side of his body. Was he just imagining it? He glanced over at Jody and noticed two small lumps appearing underneath her sapphire-blue tank top. It wasn't cold in the house. It would appear he wasn't imagining it at all.

What would she do, Christian wondered as they stood in the hallway, if he were to turn her towards him, bring her to him and claim her with his mouth? Would she struggle and push him away, or would she lean into the kiss? Claim him right back?

His palms itched to feel her skin. His lips tingled with anticipation. His mind cautioned him against being rash. There was something between them. He could see that. Feel it. Jody knew it too. Her face had angled towards him, as if waiting for him to do something. Make some kind of move.

He dropped her hand. He didn't want to push. Not because he didn't want to feel as though he'd forced anything on Jody. He suspected no one could make her do anything she wasn't one hundred per cent sure about. In truth, he was the one being cautious. In the few short days they'd known each other she'd shown him the kind of life he'd never had. A life where you weren't used to make another person look better, but were loved for who you were. Unconditionally. And if those bricks squishing his heart whenever he thought about leaving were anything to go by, some part of him craved that life. And that scared him.

'Shall we find the kitchen and make a cup of tea?' he asked, mentally kicking himself in the shins as Jody's brow furrowed in confusion. Or was it disappointment?

'Well, a cup of tea in the kitchen has to be better than just standing in the hallway like two stunned mullets,' Jody deadpanned, then took off down the hall, opening doors, poking her head in then out, shutting them, until she reached a door at the end of the hall, opened it, and disappeared.

So she was pissed at him? Well, that made two of them.

Jody busied herself at the kitchen counter spooning sugar into two mugs as the kettle boiled away. For one second, back in the hallway, she could have sworn Christian was going to kiss her. And she'd wanted him to. Hoped he would. Tingles of anticipation had swarmed over her skin, and her head had spun with desire. And then he'd dropped her hand. Gone all cold fish. Which was probably for the best. But still…

Footsteps shuffling down the hall alerted her to Christian's presence.

'So you found the kitchen.'

'Yup.' She picked up the kettle and poured hot water over the two teabags.

'And you've made the tea.'

'Aha.' She watched the rusty colour of the tea embrace the water.

'I'm sorry.'

She caught a whiff of his lemony fresh scent as he stepped closer.

'What are you sorry for?' Jody grabbed the milk and tipped it into the mugs.

'For whatever I've done to annoy you just now.'

'You don't know?' She turned around, bracing herself against the bench.

'I think I know, but I think it's better we keep things…professional.' The words were right, but his hands were open, reaching. For her. As if his mind and his body were waging a war against each other.

She knew the feeling. Even when he'd annoyed her by traipsing all over her authority back in Rabbits Leap and organising this trip without consulting her, she'd struggled. Half of her wanting him out of her life so she could go back to it. Safe. Staid. Boring. The other half knowing his visit would soon end, his job

123

would be done. He'd be gone. Leaving her. And her life would go back to what it was. Safe. Staid. Boring.

Part of her wanted her pre-Christian life back. The other part already mourned his loss.

She'd lost so much already. Her mother. Her father. Her youth. Her dreams. She knew keeping Christian at a distance was for the best. You couldn't mourn what you'd never had. And yet she still wanted to grab those outstretched hands and hold them in hers.

'It's okay...' She crossed her arms and hoped he saw the action for what it was. A way of saying 'back off'. 'Ignore me, I'm fine. I just... I guess being here has rattled me. Memories and all that.' She ducked her head as tears blurred her vision. He didn't need to know how giving up yet another thing she wanted wrenched her heart. 'I guess even time can't help you get over the loss of someone you love. No matter what the great "they" say.'

No words came from Christian. Jody wasn't surprised. What did he know about losing those you loved? 'I'm guessing you don't know anything about that, Christian? That you're one of the lucky ones who has yet to experience tragedy? Loss?' She blinked away the tears and glanced up.

Christian's Adam's apple bobbed in his neck. He went to say something. Stopped himself. His gaze shifted, his focus moving to the window. Did he see the tiled patio, with its ornate table setting for two, and wine barrels filled with begonias?

'Loss comes in many forms. It doesn't have to be about death. It can be about rejection. And those nearest to me rejected me years ago.' Christian tore his unseeing eyes from the window and turned to Jody. 'Though, to be honest, I don't see any point dwelling on the past. If you focus too much on failure it can drag you down. Drown you.'

The words were brave, though there was a waver to them, suggesting he didn't really mean or believe them. Jody stepped forward and laid a hand on Christian's bare forearm. 'I'm sorry to hear things haven't always been great for you, Christian. Truly.'

Christian shrugged her hand off, strode to the back door, flicked the lock and stepped into the doorway that led to the patio, his shoulders rising and falling as if he were trying to control his emotions. And failing. 'It doesn't matter. It's like I said – it's the past. You can't change the past, can you? You can't change the loss of your mother. Of your father. Or the moment you met a man who would eventually give you two beautiful, lively, funny boys. Those events are what they are. They are set in stone. The only thing we can do is move on. Move forward. Aim to be our best.' He stepped outside, allowing the sun to stream in where seconds before a dark shadow had stood.

Jody turned back to the cups of tea, cooling on the bench. She couldn't leave Christian like this. So obviously upset. He might not want to talk about whatever he was clearly not remotely over, but she could at least be there for him in case he changed his mind. Picking up the tea, she went out to the patio where he'd settled himself on the concrete paving stones, his knees pulled up to his chest, his arms wrapped around himself, and his jawline, set to rock-hard, telling her to keep her distance. She set the tea down in front of him and settled herself into the chair behind him.

She couldn't be with him. Wouldn't let herself. But the least she could do was be there for him.

CHAPTER NINE

Jody eyed the dresses she'd brought for the evening's excursion. Were they too casual? Not casual enough? More importantly, what had happened to Christian that, despite his show of stoicism, he was clearly still hurting from? Even with his back to her, shutting her out, she could hear the pain in his voice. He could hide behind his job, behind his perfectly pressed trousers, fashionably hued polo shirts and fancy haircut, but he couldn't hide how scarred he was by the rejection of those who should be closest. Jody guessed when he said 'nearest' he meant his family, which explained the tension she'd sensed when they'd discussed his family at lunch that day. But that didn't explain what had happened to make things go so wrong between them, and he obviously needed to talk about it. Perhaps she could push him to talk, to free himself from his pain, on their date that evening.

Wait. What? Date? Nooooo. She pushed the word out of her brain. This was no date. It was a business meeting. At a bar. With music. And drinks. And her in one of the nicest dresses she owned. Oh God. It was pretty much a date. Otherwise she'd have brought clothing that was a whole lot less showy.

She glanced at the frocks in front of her. An emerald-green silk sheath, a spaghetti-strapped flippy-hemmed yellow sundress, and a black tank dress, basic from the front but with a back that dipped down towards her butt. These weren't business-affair dresses. She'd been kidding herself they were. And which would a man like Christian prefer anyway? Something cute like the sundress, something more chic like the emerald dress, or something sexy like the black one? Jody sighed. She was going to need advice and she only had one friend who'd experienced life outside of a tiny village.

She picked up her phone and dialled.

'Jody, what's up?' Serena's usually sing-song voice sounded subdued.

'I... Well... Is this a good time? You sound distracted.'

'No, I'm not. Well... I was. But I'd rather be distracted with something else, and you make for an excellent distraction. So what's up?'

Jody sank down onto the single bed and stared at the pale-lemon-painted wall opposite. 'What does one wear when spending time with a man?'

'A man? Really? Are we talking a date kind of situation? You and the event manager guy? Does that mean he's not the overbearing pillock who thinks he knows everything that Mrs Harper insists he is?'

Jody laughed. 'Oddly enough, he's anything but. It's not a date, though. It's just a…night out, to see and hopefully confirm a band for the festival. You know… a one-time thing.'

Serena let out a squawk. 'A one-time thing? Does that translate into a one-night stand? But a classy one? Dinner, dancing, a little bedroom rumba…'

'Honestly, it's not going to be that,' Jody protested. 'Well, maybe it is, but it can't be anything more than that. It can only be… I don't know…a little fun? I mean it's not like I meet men like him every day. He's thoughtful, a good conversationalist…'

'Handsome…if you're into that clean-cut metro thing,' Serena interjected.

'Well…yeah, there is that.'

'So he ticks your boxes. So what's the problem?'

Jody paused. How was she going to explain to Serena her fear of falling for someone, of trusting her life, her heart, to someone else? How that one simple act of letting another person in could throw her whole life and the boys' lives into chaos if it went wrong. How could she explain that she didn't know whether her soul could handle one more rejection if and when everything went wrong?

'Jody…' Serena's voice was soft, yet stern. 'I think I understand what the problem is. Your mum passing, and then your dad going emotionally AWOL. You've had to be strong for so long. Be independent. I can understand that, for you, it must be hard to let someone else in, even if it is only for one night.'

Jody sucked in a breath. Serena was right. Mostly. When had her friend with her crazy former rock 'n' roll lifestyle got so wise? 'Serena, it's not just me, though. Christian's been spending time with the boys and they like him. What if they get too close? What if they're falling for him too? How will they handle it when he goes?'

'Too? So you're admitting you have fallen for him? Look, I have to be honest with you because I'm your friend, and while I'm happy to spout psycho-babble to help you deal with the past in order to have one night of fun, I don't want to see you get hurt. I'm all for this one-night thing. You need to get laid. It's been too long. But falling for him? I don't know. He's not going to stick around. He's got a life in London. Would you be willing to rip the boys away from Rabbits Leap to follow him?'

'Oh shush, I didn't say I was falling for him.' Jody gnawed at her lip, annoyed she'd put such a thought out there. It made it too real.

'You did so say that. And all I ask is that you think carefully before getting too involved. One night with a hottie? Go for it. But to hope there could be more? Just…tread carefully.'

Jody settled herself on the bed and brought her knees up to her chest. 'It's not like you to be advising people to be cautious, Serena. You've always been the "throw caution to the wind" type.'

'Yeah, well, I guess I'm getting older. Growing up. Being mature. Besides, love's not the be-all-and-end-all, is it? You've been happy with your life since going on the man-ban, haven't you?'

Jody sucked in her lower lip, inhaled, then released it. 'I have. But then you don't miss what you've never really had. And it's not like Rabbits Leap is filled with boyfriend potential. The pickings are slim.'

'Tell me about it. My mum keeps pointing out the Harper boys, but...'

'Sometimes a good-looking man isn't worth it if his mother is the world's biggest gossip, know it all, and uber-Mother Hen?'

'You know it. Besides, I'm not interested. It's too soon after...'

Jody didn't press. Serena hadn't said much since her return to Rabbits Leap about what had gone on between her and her ex. Jody figured she'd have her reasons, and they'd talk about it in Serena's own good time. She could wait. She wasn't going anywhere. Certainly not to London to follow a man who'd most likely break her heart.

'Far be it for me to tell you what to do, Jodes, but if you're really tempted to go there with this guy, maybe you should keep it light and easy. One night. Treat yourself. It's been a long time. But don't go too deep. The deeper you go, the more things hurt.'

Jody flashed back to the moment she'd woken up over a decade ago. Expecting a bright future, filled with excitement, and love, and joy. Everything she didn't have at home. Only to find an empty space beside her in bed. Not a trace of the man she'd so foolishly pinned her hopes on to be found. The tears that had followed had lasted months. Until two small boys came squalling into the world. Serena was right. The more you invested yourself in another person, the more you had to lose.

'One night.' She tested the words. Tried to decide if she was comfortable with the idea. 'One night.' Tingles tap-danced low in her stomach. One night with no expectations. That she could do.

'You sound like you've made your mind up. Now go put on a dress, something you feel comfortable in. Something easy to take off...'

Jody clapped a hand over her mouth and muffled a nervous giggle.

'...Then go and have yourself a really good night. You deserve it, my friend.'

'You're a gem, Serena. One of those Harper boys would be lucky to have you,' Jody teased.

'Oh, shush. You know that's never going to happen.' Serena laughed. 'Night, night, Jodes, don't sleep tight.'

*　*　*

Christian fussed with his hair in front of the bathroom mirror. Artfully tossing it one way, then shoving it the opposite way in irritation. What was going on with him? Was he nervous? Of going out for a work event? With a woman he found not only incredibly hot, but who, that afternoon, had shown him such simple kindness and patience. Not probing or prying, but

132

simply sitting near him until he'd cleared his head of the guilt and disappointment, untangled his arms and legs and come to sit with her – again in silence – until he was ready to speak.

And when he spoke it had been about the weather, about work, about anything and everything except his family. And she'd been cool with that. Accepting. Of him.

Warmth flooded his gut. It had been a long time since he'd felt accepted by anyone. Or had anyone show him compassion. Consideration. His own fault, really, as he'd built a supposedly indestructible wall around himself. Emblazoned 'keep out' on it. Yet Jody had somehow scrubbed that sign right out. Cut a door into the wall, let herself in and, whether she knew it or not, was showing him another kind of life. Perhaps a better one. No wonder he was...

He fingered the collar of his T-shirt. Did it feel this tight a second ago? When had it begun to choke him? And was a moss-green T-shirt all that attractive? Maybe he should've gone with a navy-blue one? What about footwear? Boat shoes or loafers? Geez, at this rate he'd be questioning his choice of underwear. Thank God he'd only brought a couple of pairs of identical black boxer briefs. That was at least one thing he didn't have to consider.

Three raps in quick succession stopped his sartorial-stressing in its tracks. 'Are you going to be long in there? There's only one bathroom...and, well...'

Jody didn't need to continue for Christian to figure out what she was on about. 'Oh yes. Sorry. I'll be out in a second.' He turned back to the mirror, mussed his hair one more time and gave himself a stern nod. *You're fine. You look fine. It's not a date, so everything is fine.*

He turned and opened the door, then wilted against the doorjamb as all his confidence and bravado was stripped away by the sight before him. 'Oh.'

'Do I look okay? Am I dressed appropriately?' Jody tugged at the hem of her little black dress, which clung at mid thigh, then rearranged the neckline, lifting it a little higher. 'Giddy aunt, I'm overdressed, aren't I? Totally inappropriate to see a band in a bar. I look ridiculous. I'll do what I need to do here, and then I'll go change.'

'No. Don't.' Christian reached out and caught Jody's hand. 'You look amazing. Perfect. I'll be the envy of men everywhere having you next to me.'

Jody glowed at the compliment and stood a little taller. Or was it those heels? Those very sexy, black-leather, six-inch heels? He pushed himself off the doorjamb to get the measure of her height. Her lips were now nigh on equal with his. Pink, full, with a subtle shine. And completely kissable.

'So I should keep this dress on then?' She skirted past him, her bare arm brushing his. The hair on his forearms stood to attention. Just as something else had been trying to, ever since he'd got an eyeful of the back of the dress. Black fabric was replaced by a stunning sweep of glorious satiny skin. Christian gave a quick nod and turned away so she couldn't see the campsite setting up shop in his groin area. 'I'll meet you downstairs,' he called as she shut the bathroom door.

Taking the stairs two at a time he began to pace back and forth in the hallway. *Think unsexy thoughts. Think crocodiles in bright-pink pyjamas. Think about your nanna with her teeth out, placed next to her at the dinner table.*

Think long, tanned and toned legs wrapped around your waist.

Christian raced to the kitchen. He had to sort himself out before Jody came back down. There was no way he wanted her to see him like this. So... uncool. That was it! He needed to cool down. Yanking open the freezer door he searched for what he was looking for. Scooping it up with one hand, he pulled out the waistband of his trousers and underwear with the other, and dropped the contents into the pouch he'd created.

'Oh my God,' he squeaked, clapping his hand over his mouth as he hopped about the kitchen. What had he been thinking dropping ice cubes down there? Was he crazy? Yes, he was. Crazy with lust. He'd had to do something to curb it. And curb it he had. The erected tent had been levelled. Something wet dribbled down his leg. He glanced down to see a wet patch spreading over the front of his camel-coloured trousers. *Shit!*

How was he going to fix this? He didn't have time to put on another pair. That would look weird. But if he left things as they were, Jody would want to know why he had water dribbling out of his pants.

The clickety-clack of heels on the wooden staircase sent his racing heart into potential heart-attack zone.

There was only one thing for it.

He went to the sink, grabbed a water glass from the cupboard next to it, filled it with water and splashed it over the existing wet patch. 'Shit!' he exclaimed, just as Jody entered the room.

'What's happened? How'd you manage that? Quick, get a tea towel before it spreads further.' She snatched up the tea towel hanging over a dining chair, rushed forward and pressed it onto the offending water stain.

'Um… Jody…that's…um…' Christian stammered. *Double shit.* Apparently the happy camper was stirring back into life. 'I…can…take…over.' He swatted her hand away and pressed the tea towel onto his groin.

Jody backed away, her cheeks flaming. 'I didn't think… I'm so sorry… Do you think the floor might be kind enough to open up and swallow me whole?'

Christian pressed hard, soaking up the water while praying for his downstairs operation to behave. 'If it can, I hope it swallows both of us.' With things feeling settled, Christian removed the tea towel. 'It's a bit obvious, don't you think?'

'Erm.' Jody's cheeks glowed to the point he feared they'd set alight.

It would seem something else had been obvious to her.

'I think it'll dry as we walk. It's a warm night.' She fanned herself. 'Really warm. Almost too hot too handle.' A giggle, verging on hysterical, escaped her parted lips.

At least she wasn't disappointed with what little action had been going on in his trousers. Though how would she be acting if she'd experienced the whole pre-ice hog? Would she be giggling? Hyperventilating? Or would they have been late to the bar? Christian tossed the tea towel on the dining-room table. It wasn't worth thinking about. What was worth thinking about was how radiant Jody was when she laughed. And how her eyes were sparkling with good humour, and something else he couldn't quite put his finger on... but it looked a little like she'd decided on something. Could that something be him?

He crooked his arm and cocked his head. 'Shall we walk, m'lady?'

Jody hooked her arm companionably through his. 'Indeed we shall. And don't let go, because I'm not sure I can walk any sort of distance in these monstrosities.'

Let go? Not in a million years. Not if he had any say in it.

CHAPTER TEN

Fairy lights dripped from the ceiling. Every table flickered with LED flameless candles. Not as romantic as the real deal, but entrancing nonetheless. The setting sun cast its magic light over the customers who'd come to dine, dance and drink. And the man next to her kept casting his eyes up and down her body in a way that made Jody feel every bit as brilliant as the sun's final rays.

'This place is amazing.' She squeezed Christian's upper arm and took a moment to appreciate his muscled bicep. Not too big, not too small. The perfect size, leading her to believe he could lift her up against a wall and hold her as he… She swallowed. Now was not the time to be getting hot and flustered. Work first. Play, hopefully, later.

'It really is. It's a pity the festival finishes before dark. Fairy lights dripping off Rabbits Leap's main street buildings would look quite amazing. Or coloured lights criss-crossing the street.'

Disappointment hit Jody hurricane-force in the gut, and she unhooked her hand from his arm. So he was back to being Mr Event Manager. Fair enough. But still... After chatting with Serena, and having that moment by the bathroom, then in the kitchen, followed by their easy conversation on the way to the bar, she'd dared to believe she might be able to scratch the itch that reared up whenever she was in Christian's presence.

'Maybe we could do it for the next festival? Start it later. Finish it later. What do you think?' He cocked his head to the side, his lips pursed in thought.

'The next time? You'd come back? Even if it meant dealing with the two Mrs Hs?'

'As long as you're around to keep them in line.'

Jody gave a light snort. 'As if I keep them in line. There's a reason I hired you, remember?'

Christian nodded at the barman. 'Well, I'm glad you did. Now, what would you like to drink?'

'Oh, just a white wine spritzer, please.'

'Jody, you don't have two young lads to get up for tomorrow morning. You can sleep in. Live dangerously. Have a white wine. No spritz.'

Jody lifted herself up onto a bar stool, cupped her chin in her hand and flashed Christian a grin. 'Are you trying to get me tipsy, Mr Middlemore?'

Christian slapped his hand to his chest, his eyes widening in mock-horror. 'Me? Do a thing like that? Not at all. It was just a suggestion.' He turned to the barman. 'I'll have a pint of lager. And the lady will have a white wine sprit—'

Jody laid her hand on Christian's forearm. 'A sauvignon blanc, please.' She nodded her thanks to the barman and returned her gaze to Christian. 'If I have a headache tomorrow, you're taking me out for a big greasy brunch. Bacon. Eggs. Sausages. Thickly buttered toast. Grilled tomatoes. The lot.'

'Deal.' Christian paid for the drinks and took a sip of his beer. He set his glass down and Jody repressed a giggle when she saw his upper lip was rimmed with froth.

Not thinking to ask permission, she reached up and ran her thumb around the foam, removing it. An image rose unbidden of her thumb between Christian's lips. Being sucked upon. His tongue running over her thumb pad, tasting. Tantalising.

Jody pulled her hand away as a flush stormed her body, from the tips of her toes to the roots of her hair. 'Sorry.' She picked up her wine and took a gulp, then set the glass down a little too hard, sending a small tsunami of wine up and over the rim. 'Terrible habit. I do the same to the boys when they have a milk-moustache. I'll probably be doing it to them when they're our age…'

Christian swiped the back of his hand around his mouth, then pulled it away for an inspection. 'Well, you're good at your job. Not a speck left. See?' He twisted his hand round for her to see.

'Good. Well. That's that sorted. What happens next?' She craned her neck to check out the small stage where the band was setting up. 'They look to be a way away from playing. Shall we have something to eat? I'm a bit hungry.' She clutched her belly as it rumbled its agreement.

Christian stared at her stomach. 'God, I heard that. Even over this crowd. You must be starving. Do you want to grab a table and I'll order some burgers?'

'Please. Make mine chicken.' Jody slid off her stool, clutched her wine between her thumb and forefinger and wove her way to a table for two that had opened up at the front of the bar. A little away from the main crowd so they could talk, while enjoying an expansive view of the sea. At least if the conversation stalled they could admire the scene before them.

'Great table.' Christian slid into the chair opposite hers. 'Nice work nabbing it.'

Jody shrugged and took another sip of wine. She eyed the glass, already half empty. At this rate she'd be three sheets to the wind and Christian would have to carry her home. 'So...' Jody ran her finger around the rim of her glass as she searched for an easy topic to chat about. 'Tell me, what do you love most about being an event manager?'

Christian leant back in his chair, his eyes dancing with laughter. 'So you've finally decided to interview me properly? You're a few days late, you know.'

141

Jody rolled her eyes. 'No. I'm just being interested. It's not like you meet an event manager every day of your life. At least, not in Rabbits Leap. It's all farmers and families.'

'And butchers. And publicans. And café owners. And I hear there's a pretty excellent artist in the area too.' Christian winked.

'Oh, she's pretty?' Jody anchored her elbow on the table and rested her chin on her fist.

'It's just what I've heard…' Christian smirked. 'And to answer your question, what I love about my job is seeing people happy. The looks on their faces when they're wandering the streets hand in hand, taking in the sights and sounds of a fair. The way a crowd sways and sings as one when a singer is performing their favourite song. It makes the early starts, the late nights, the middle-of-the-night calls and the stress worth it.'

'I still can't believe you agreed to help us out. It's like fate smiled on the town. On me…'

'Yes, well…I'm starting to feel the same way.' Christian reached for Jody's hand. His eyes, soft yet intent upon her, sent a peppering of goosebumps over her skin. 'You know, I wasn't sure if taking on this festival was the right thing to do. I wondered if I'd get bored.'

'Geez, thanks.' Jody pulled her hand away and tucked it under her thigh.

'No, hear me out. You see, it's not as full-on as what I usually do. I'm used to a frenetic pace. I don't do relaxing. Hell, relaxing is considered a dirty word

142

in my family. But I've found myself enjoying my time in Rabbits Leap. Sleeping eight hours a night. Eating proper meals rather than snatching whatever's fast and easy to throw down my throat while I'm racing between appointments. I've liked our collaborative approach. And Lord knows the villagers are nowhere near as high-maintenance as the people I'm used to dealing with.'

Jody snickered. 'Um, have you forgotten about Mrs Hunter and Mrs Harper?'

Christian's lips turned up ever so slightly. 'They're not that bad. You know that band...' He mouthed the name of a popular rock band.

Jody nodded.

'They take the title of high-maintenance and then some. A special room was required for each of the five members. One of them wanted a pet leopard to be installed in their room. Another insisted on a pyramid of three hundred and two cupcakes, then pitched a fit when it was three hundred and three. Another wanted a catwalk featuring a steady stream of models, both men and women, wearing costumes from different eras, parading down it. I loved the challenge. Revelled in it. But I could've slept for a week after they left. Not that I did. Another day, another event.' The corners of his lips turned down again. 'It's a great job, but there are those moments when I feel people are waiting to see me fail.'

'Why would anyone want to see you fail? How's that helpful? I mean, I get the feeling that, back in London, you're a pain in the arse to work for. You had me quit on the first day, remember?' She grinned at the memory. 'I'm glad you got me back, though.'

'So am I. You're a good person, Jody. A good friend.'

'A friend? Is that how you see me?' Jody pushed her plate away, the hunger that had been gnawing at her stomach replaced by something that felt disconcertingly like disappointment. What had she wanted him to say? Lover? Girlfriend? Soulmate?

Christian followed her lead and pushed his burger to the side. He reached for his beer and took a long glug. 'Not all people are as good as you, Jody. Let's be honest, there are only so many big events to go around, and if I were to ever have a major screw-up there would be about five people I can think of who'd gladly step into my shoes.' Christian paused, a shadow crossing his face. 'Ugh, all this talk of failure has done a number on my appetite. But what's that saying? There's a meal in every beer? I'll just have to order another.'

'And get me another wine while you're at it.' Jody picked up her glass, necked the wine and passed him the empty vessel. If things weren't going to get lusty she might as well take advantage of her one night of freedom and get a little lushy.

She kept track of Christian's broad shoulders as he disappeared into the crowd of merry punters. Why was a man as successful as Christian so afraid of making mistakes? Sure, he'd had a rough start when he got to Rabbits Leap. But once he'd realised the villagers weren't the type to take orders but were happy to work in collaboration he'd come right. Had that rough start put the wind up him? Shaken his faith in himself? Maybe it was time to make Christian feel better about himself. Tell him the tale of a girl who made a mistake, but believed it could be rectified.

A glass of wine was set in front of her, followed by the dull clunk of a pint glass on the wooden table.

'I'm back.' Christian sank into his seat. 'Though I guess that's obvious.'

'Indeed,' Jody murmured and took another gulp of wine. Dutch courage. 'It was me who broke the pool,' she blurted, dropping her gaze to her lap. 'I did it. Me. When I was younger. That's why I'm determined to make this festival every bit as good as it can be. That's why I hired you with my own money. I need to say sorry to the town without them ever knowing it was me who broke the pool in the first place.' Jody's heart pitter-pattered, like a thousand ants were marching across it in formation. Her hands twisted around each other, nerves stretching tauter by the second. Why wasn't he saying something? 'Don't just sit there. Yell at me. Tell me how horrible I am. Worst human ever. You should probably put me in the stocks and have people throw rotten fruit at me. It could be a stall at the festival. It'd make a ton of money. We could save the pool and build another for good measure.' She paused, waiting for the recriminations to fly. They didn't. 'Aren't you going to say something? Anything?' she screeched, wincing at the high-pitched whine coming from her mouth.

She dared glance up to see Christian bent over in his chair. His shoulders shaking. His face buried in his hands. She'd made him cry? He was crying at her pain? What the hell was going on?

'Christian?' She bolted out of her chair and rushed to his side and began to rub his back in calming little circles. 'Are you okay? Are you hurt? Have you choked on a chip? God, I'm sorry. I know it's a big confession. But it shouldn't be a life-threatening one. Death by chip. What a terrible way to go.' She thumped on his back for good measure.

The intensity of Christian's shaking reached quaking levels.

'Christian? Look at me. Breathe. Am I going to have to call a doctor?'

His back rose. Fell. Rose again. Fell again. He was taking deep breaths as directed. Good. Excellent. His head lifted. Tears streaked his cheeks. But the frown had been replaced by a wide-mouthed grin. His eyes shined with amusement.

The band's drummer began to bash out a beat, joined by the jangle of electric guitar, the thrum of bass, and the happy crooning of the singer.

Christian grabbed her hand. 'I need to know more about this pool-breakage. I want to hear the whole story. Later. But first, we need to dance.'

Jody, confused, yet catching on to his infectious amusement, allowed herself to be pulled onto the dance floor.

***

Christian breathed in the vanilla-sweet scent of Jody's hair. Her head was nestled upon his shoulder as they slow-danced to an old-school rock 'n' roll ballad. Only moments before, they'd been spinning and twirling to a high-paced number. Never had he seen her more beautiful than with her head thrown back as he spun her in and out, over and over again, a raucous laugh escaping those crazy, kissable lips, bringing smiles to the faces of their fellow dancers. And the whole time she'd focused on him. Only him. Not once did her eyes slip to check out the other people on the dance floor. It was as if tonight Jody belonged to him.

If only tonight could last for ever.

He inhaled sharply, causing Jody to lift her head, to search his face with enquiring eyes.

'What's wrong?' she asked. Taking a small step back. Creating space between them.

He pulled her back into his embrace. He didn't want to experience space from Jody. He wanted to keep her close. As she'd confessed her wrongdoing, self-disgust radiating off her, he'd realised how much he wanted her. All of her. Never had he met someone so good and strong. So just. Jody didn't slide through life ignoring her mistakes in the hope of making them disappear; she worked to put the wrongs right. And perhaps, just maybe, meeting her was life's way of showing him how he could right his wrongs. For the first time since he'd realised he was to blame for the pop star, Madam

Foxy, becoming ill, he wasn't furious with himself. Mistakes happened. You could only apologise, right your wrongs and move on. He'd call her management tomorrow and set things straight. The only thing worse than getting something wrong was waiting for his world to fall apart. At least this way, if it was going to fall apart, it would be on his terms.

'Nothing's wrong. Tonight's been perfect.' He took a lock of her hair in his hand, curled it around his finger, then tucked it behind her ear. 'You're perfect.' His hand caressed the top of her bare back. Soft. Smooth. And incredibly sexy.

Her lips parted, her tongue darted out and licked her lips. Her chest hitched against his as if she were going to say something, then stopped herself. A slow smile lit up her face. Her head tilted back a touch, giving access. Giving permission?

And just like that, her lips pressed upon his. Warm. Lush. Her hand fisted itself into his hair and pulled him down, their lips fusing. Her honeyed scent surrounded him, intoxicated him, and he melted into the kiss. Asked for more. And she gave. Opening her mouth to him, allowing him to taste her. Sweet. Tangy. The kiss deepened, their tongues entwined. Jody moaned into his mouth, pressed up against him. He ran his hand down the length of her spine, enjoying the way she squirmed under his touch. He caressed the curve of her arse, as toned and round as he'd imagined. Oh God, he wanted her. Now.

He wanted her to be with him, twisted around him, on him. He wanted to kiss away their memories of embarrassment, of failure. He wanted to create newer, better memories. Memories that would fight off the desolation that wrapped around him when he thought about his worst failure. The failure to please his parents. To work his way into their hearts.

Somewhere in the distance a crowd cheered and clapped. A slap on the back brought him to his senses and he broke the kiss. The crowd were clapping and cheering for them. The band had stopped, but he and Jody hadn't noticed. Wrapped up in their own sweet music, they'd continued to sway against each other. Continued to explore each other.

Jody ducked her head, but she couldn't hide her flaming cheeks.

'Show's over, folks.' Christian laughed, and flapped his hands, shooing people away. Taking Jody by the hand he led her to the band, who were packing up. 'Great set, guys. Do you think you could work that magic on the people of Rabbits Leap?'

The lead singer threw his curly-haired head back and chuckled. 'We sure can, but you may need to give the festival an adult rating from what we saw happen on that dance floor.'

Christian glanced at Jody, whose face was half hidden as she burrowed into his bicep in embarrassment. 'I'm sure we can control ourselves, if only while you're playing at the festival. Right, Jody?'

His heart soared when she smiled. After that kiss on the dance floor, he'd dared to hope she was up for breaking her one rule, even if only for one night. But something in that smile made him think she might break her biggest rule, not once, but for forever.

CHAPTER ELEVEN

'You were amazing back there.' Jody half walked, half skipped, barefoot as they walked hand in hand towards the flat, her heels dangling from her other hand, bouncing against her leg with every step. 'I can't believe the band were happy to do it for half the price. I didn't even have to say two words. Which is great because I was so flustered I couldn't have got two words out anyway.'

Christian squeezed her hand and tugged her closer. 'Well, I think name-dropping some of the festivals I've worked on in London helped. They're probably hoping I'll put a good word in for them when it comes time to book bands down the track.'

'Well, you would, wouldn't you?'

'Of course I would. I may be tone deaf but I have some rhythm, and they've that in spades, so even I know they're seriously great. We're lucky to have them. I haven't danced like that in years.'

'I haven't kissed like that in years.' Jody pushed open the gate and walked up the garden path, each step

151

filling her with anticipation. 'You're a talented kisser, you know that?'

'Says she who just admitted she's not been kissed for years. You've probably forgotten what it's like to be kissed. I could be as good as a frog at kissing.'

'Well, there was that one frog who was actually a prince. And he got a woman to kiss him. Maybe you're a bit like that?'

'A rare breed of frog who can kiss well?'

Jody tickled his waist, laughing as he let out a squeak. 'I may have been out of the game for a while, but it doesn't mean I've forgotten how to play.' Jody peered down at her toes, afraid to look Christian in the eye. Her words were meant to have been light-hearted, joking banter. But they'd come out intense. Sensual. A challenge to herself. If she dared look up at Christian, would she see an acceptance of that challenge? Could she, would she, follow through with things if she did?

They arrived at the door. Faced it, still hand in hand. Neither one saying a word. The air between them shimmered with a mixture of playfulness and desire. A heady combination. Fingertips touched her cheek, gently turned her head, then slid down to her chin, tipping her face up to meet his gaze, her breath catching in her throat as he searched her face as if seeking something. Permission? Affirmation?

'I think we should have a nightcap, don't you?' Jody whispered. Nerves erasing her brief bravery. It had been so long. Too long. Would she know what to do? Would he find her wanting? She'd forgone the wild and free years so many women in their twenties experienced in order to do the best job she could raising her boys. She hadn't been able to justify spending money on the magazines that told girls 'how to make a man beg for more in ten easy steps', or 'how to lick, sip and suck him until he screams'. That money went into the boys' clothes and whatever hobbies they were into at the time. Karate. Guitar. Comic-book collecting.

Christian pulled the key out of his pocket. 'I think a nightcap is a great idea.'

He pushed opened the door. 'Ladies before lads.'

She let go of his hand and stepped past, keeping distance between them. Afraid of how she'd feel, what she'd do, if his bare skin touched hers. She could feel his eyes on her back. Ripples of goosebumps raced over her. Why had she chosen this dress? It was too sexy. Too look-at-me. The sheath would have been better. More businesslike, less likely to get her in trouble. The black dress was a dress made to be taken off, slipped from shoulders, pushed down past a waist. The sheath was a barrier. It said 'no blokes allowed'.

She entered the kitchen and fussed about putting water into the kettle and washing out their mugs from earlier.

There was a clink of glass behind her. A dull thud. 'I was thinking a whiskey might be a nice way to end the evening?' Christian removed the crystal stopper

153

from the decanter and sloshed two generous pours into matching cut-crystal glasses. He held a glass out to her. 'Not trying to get you drunk. It's just that it's a mild night, and it's been an enjoyable one too. I thought a whiskey under the moonlight in the courtyard would be the perfect way to round things off.'

'Sure. Sounds great.' Jody reached for the glass. Her fingertips caressed Christian's, sending a jangle of excitement racing through her body. *Get a grip, woman*, she growled at herself. He was just a man. A good-looking man. A charming man. A thoughtful man. But he was just a man. And as much as she'd been tempted to do something more than kiss him earlier, she wasn't so sure about it now. Not because she didn't want to. But because there were too many 'what ifs' involved.

What if, despite her lack of experience, it was good?

What if she loved it too much?

What if she wanted more?

More frightening, what if Christian wanted more?

What if he hated her when she said she couldn't give him that?

She followed him out to the table and perched on the edge of the chair. She couldn't give one hundred per cent of herself to Christian, not even fifty per cent, not when she'd vowed to give all of herself to the boys. To give them the attention she'd never received as a child. The care. The love. Adding a man into the mix would be a distraction. And she knew all too well how being ignored by the person who's meant to love you most hurt. How it made you do things you wouldn't usually do. Rash things.

'So, tell me, Jody McArthur…' Christian shot her a mischievous grin. 'How did a fine, upstanding citizen such as yourself, come to break the Rabbits Leap pool? And how did you do it?'

And there he was, doing a Ms Millie on her. Reading her thoughts. But unlike Ms Millie, who never asked for your opinion or thoughts, just stated how she saw things as fact before moseying on her merry way, Christian wanted to know more. He was actually interested in her, as a person. A warm glow filled her that could have been down to the whiskey, except that she'd yet to take a sip.

'Oh, you know…' She waved her hand about airily, not keen to disclose the finer details of her past. 'Just pitched a teenage fit and decided to take it out on the pool. It was a stupid thing to do.'

'But why the pool? Why not, I don't know, get drunk and vomit all through your sheets. Or steal the family car and go joyriding. What was it about the pool that enraged you to the point you decided to destroy it?'

Jody brought her knees up to her chest. A barrier against the questions.

'And…' Christian continued. 'How did you get away with it? Surely someone would know something in a town as small as that. Like your brother? Or that friend of yours… Serena is it?'

'Why do you want to know?' Jody asked, hoping if she were defensive enough he'd back off. 'It's not like you were the one who couldn't swim in the pool. And it's not like that moment defined me as a human being. I've not put a foot out of line since.'

Christian raised his eyebrows, his lips morphing into a quirk.

'Well, apart from get tipsy, have sex and make babies with a complete stranger. But I don't regret that. I can't. It is what it is. And besides, those boys of mine are the best thing that ever happened to me. Before they came along my life was lonely as all hell.' *Shit*. She sank her top teeth into her lower lip. She'd said too much, and just gone and given Christian another thread of her life to unravel.

'I can't imagine you lonely. You seem to be surrounded by people who care for you, who love you.' He swirled the amber liquid around in the glass and took a sip.

Jody followed suit. If things were about to get personal she'd need all the lip-loosening liquid she could get. 'Well it didn't always feel that way.'

'Why? Were you hard work as a teen? Did you push people away?'

A bitter laugh filled the courtyard. 'No. The opposite. I wanted people around me, but they weren't always available. Emotionally anyway.'

'Serena? She strikes me as being very emotionally available.'

'She wasn't there. Convinced her parents to send her to boarding school in the city. And Tony was busy being a teenage boy. Stayed in his room a lot. Played video games. The most amount of communication I could get out of him was the odd grunt.'

'And your dad?' Christian set the glass on the table and leant forward, his elbows resting on his knees, his hands clasped together.

Jody's heart twinged, as it always did when she thought about her father. Their relationship. Or lack thereof. 'Dad and I… We weren't close.' Jody swallowed to try and budge the lump that had formed in her throat. It didn't give an inch. She took another mouthful of whiskey. The lump dissolved a little, enough that she could talk. 'He was devastated after Mum died. She was his world. So was the pub. And when she died he shut me out. And Tony. It was the pub all the time.' Jody tipped her head towards the moon. It blurred as tears threatened to spill. 'I'd hoped with time he'd come round. That he'd make space in his heart for us, but he never did. So I started acting out. Broke into the old sweet shop and filled my pockets with whatever was handy. Tony eventually joined me on those escapades. Back then it was the most bonding we did.' She blinked to clear the tears. The memory of her and Tony jimmying open the door of what was now Mel's Café making her smile. They'd not been caught, not once. 'Do you know that made the front of the local paper? We were called "The Treat Thief". They even set up a camera to catch the culprit. I heard the owner tell Dad they were planning to do it, so Tony and I just made sure to stay down, to crawl army-style over the floor and go for the sweets on the bottom shelf.'

'Who knew behind that angelic face was a hardened criminal?' Christian's low voice, soft and teasing, caring too, caressed her. Gave her the courage to go on.

'I also snuck out at night and went for long rambles all over the fields. Stole a fair few eggs from local farms. Stole the town sign and hung it above my bed. Dad saw it, told me to return it and that was it. Not a flicker of anything that would indicate he cared about what I got up to.' Damn it. The moon was blurring again. Jody took another sip of the warming drink, hoping it could put some heat into her beaten soul.

'So how did the pool come about? Details. I want them all. No skimping.' An ear-piercing scritch filled the air as metal scraped on paving stones. Something encased Jody's hands. She glanced down to find Christian's hands around hers. Protective. Strong. Present.

She took a deep breath. If she was going to disclose her greatest shame, her worst moment, she was only going to do it once, and she was going to do it right. 'It was after the sign-stealing. I was angry. Hurt. And so very disappointed. I was sixteen, surrounded by people who seemed to have caring families. Mothers and fathers who asked after them, who came to school productions and sports days, who made sure there was a hot meal on the table at night and a decent lunch to take to school. I couldn't understand why they had that whole American sitcom happy family life going on and I didn't. Why did I have the mother who died? Why did I have a father who didn't care where I was

158

or what I did?' Jody clucked her tongue. 'God, I sound like a spoilt brat, don't I? Poor me, poor me, poor me. Sorry.'

Christian's hands pressed firmly against hers. 'You sound like you were wounded. And frankly, I don't blame you for feeling the way you did. It's not... I mean... It can't be easy having your family life broken... Especially when, in your case, it was out of your control.'

Jody paused. There was something in Christian's tone that didn't ring true, as if he knew about how your life could change so totally, whether you liked it or not. Was it something to do with his earlier admission about his family not wanting him?

'Jody? Are you going to tell me what happened next... Or is it too hard? I know I wanted to hear about it, but not if you don't want to tell me. I guess sometimes it's hard to talk about the past, even if we're better off for doing so.'

And there it was again, that tone which told of knowledge of pain. Of sadness. She'd get to the bottom of that, Jody decided. Because it sounded like she wasn't the only one in need of a heart-healing confession.

She took a deep breath in, rolling her shoulders in an attempt to release some of the tension that had them all scrunched up around her ears, then relaxed. 'Where was I?'

'Post sign-stealing,' Christian prompted, inching closer so their knees were interlocked.

'So, I had hoped my father would realise the sign-stealing was a cry for help, for attention. But he didn't. Instead he acted like nothing had happened. Kept serving the beers, kept frying the chips and frozen fish, kept his smile on for the locals, only erasing it at the end of the night when he'd come upstairs to go to bed. One night I waited up for him. I'd decided we needed to hash things out. If the passage of time wasn't going to heal his heart, make him realise he had things to live for – *people* to live for – then maybe a good bollocking would. So I sat hunched on the couch watching whatever late-night drivel was on the television, until I heard the slow, tired thumps of him walking up the stairs.' Jody slipped her hands out from between Christian's and folded her arms across her chest as the memory sent a shiver through her. 'He came in and said "shouldn't you be in bed". Not a question, just a statement. He made no effort to tell me to go to bed, but that was no surprise as he never made an effort anyway. So I replied "shouldn't you be a father?".' Tears prickled her eyes and she angrily swiped them away. 'I'll never forget the way he looked. Blank. No emotion. It was like I'd just said "pass the salt" or "nice day for a walk". "Did you hear me, Dad?" I asked. Part of me hoped he was a bit deaf from all the rowdy chatter and music in the pub.' She half hiccupped, half laughed, as a sob threatened to escape. 'He told me he heard. But that blankness remained. Like he didn't care. Then he turned round and walked out of the lounge. I heard his bedroom door close, the gentlest of snicks. He didn't give enough of a shit to at least be angry, to wham the door closed. So I did. I marched out of the lounge, slamming the door behind me. Then took off out of the pub. That big oak door makes one hell of a boom. I stood in the middle of the street, waiting for him to come and check on me. Waiting for him to snap out of whatever fog he was living in. I waited until I was shivering in my nightgown, my toes going blue. Then I just thought... "stuff it".' Jody shook her head and sucked in another sob-swallowing breath. 'Actually, I thought much harsher words than that. Words I wouldn't repeat now because you've seen what happens when the boys learn new words. Cock-up being one of them.' She let out a laugh, but the sob she'd been holding down broke loose.

Strong, warm, comforting arms enveloped her. A large palm slowly rubbed the length of her back, up and down. Giving her permission to mourn the events of that night. Of her childhood.

She allowed her head to rest on Christian's shoulder, but didn't give in to the embrace, didn't return it. She needed the story to be out. Just this once. Then it could be boxed up and put back in the smallest corner of her mind's attic for the rest of time.

'I'd never felt so angry. More than angry, enraged. All I wanted to do was destroy something. To hurt someone in the way I was hurting. And I remembered the pool was due to be renovated. The changing sheds were to be painted. The pool was emptied of water so it could be refinished. And the paint was in storage ready for the work to begin. And so I ran to the swimming pool, jumped the fence and broke into the storage shed.' The tears were now flowing freely and Christian's shirt was becoming soggier by the second. 'I lugged the pails out and splashed them all over the place. On the grass. Concrete. Up the walls. Then I saw a mallet leaning up against the shed wall, one of those rubber-headed ones that don't make much noise when you whack things. Lord knows what it was doing there, but it was there. And I was still fuming. I took that thing and I... I...'

Christian shushed against her hair, his hand still stroking her back. 'You don't have to go on. I think I know what happened next.'

'But I have to. I have to tell. I've kept it inside all these years,' she whispered, lifting her head to see Christian. Expecting to see revulsion in his eyes, surprised to see kindness. 'I lowered myself into the pool, grabbed the mallet. Then I lifted it high over my head and smashed it down on the concrete. Again and again and again. Only stopping when the puff had gone out of me, and the horror and guilt of what I'd done set in. I took my anger out on the community. The very people who'd treated Tony and I so well after our mother passed away. Who did their best to keep an eye on us when our father wouldn't. They didn't deserve that, Christian. They were good people. They *are* good people. I ruined their happiness in order to lessen my unhappiness.'

'But it didn't work that way, did it?' He tucked a damp clump of hair behind her ears. 'You were still unhappy. Probably more so.'

Jody nodded. 'I was. I dropped the mallet and ran home. Tried to sneak through the back door but Dad was waiting for me. I guess he'd heard the front door slam shut just as I'd hoped.'

'Did he do anything? Say anything?' Christian's hand was cupping her face, his thumb skimming her cheek.

'No. Just saw me to my room. Without a word.'

'And kicked your arse when the vandalism was discovered?'

Jody leaned into the cupped hand, grateful for the support. And the understanding. 'He never did. He must have figured it out, though. The timing was right.'

'But how come no one else did? Rabbits Leap doesn't strike me as the kind of place to have had security cameras everywhere... Well, apart from in the sweet shop...' he smirked. 'But surely there would have been fingerprinting and someone must have heard the mallet striking the concrete. It might have had a rubber head, but they still make noise. Especially in the dead of night. I just can't believe no one looked out of their window to see a young Jody McArthur fleeing the scene of the crime.'

'Well that's where things get weird. And also fate seemed to step in. You see the workmen went in that next day and found the mess, alerted the parish council, and from what I heard from the locals chatting at the bar, they were annoyed, but they had insurance, so figured it could be fixed while the person responsible was being hunted down. Except they didn't have insurance. It turns out the town clerk had been faking payments and siphoning funds and all sorts. He must've realised his activities were about to be revealed because he took off, and when in fact they realised the amount of fraud that had gone on and that there was no insurance to pay for the pool, they refocused their energy onto searching for him and getting back what money they could.'

'And did they?' Christian released Jody and settled back into his seat, his eyes rounded in incredulity.

'No. Never did. The theory is he took off to somewhere no one would ever find him. Some say the Australian Outback. Others say the bottom of the deepest sea, the money strapped to him in an act of spite. I suspect that last one is just a bit of wishful thinking on their part.'

'So there was no money to fix the pool...'

'And it was all my fault.'

'Hence the reason you're willing to pay me out of your own money to make the festival a success.'

'Exactly. And that's why no one must ever know that the money has come from me. I want to fix my mistake, but I want to do it on my terms. If the town ever discovered what I did...' Jody shuddered, seeing the pitchforks stabbed in her direction...

'They'd never forgive you.'

'Not after everything they've done for me, for us. I'd be banished from my home. At the very least I'd be an outcast. And the boys would suffer.'

'Well, your secret is safe with me.' Christian placed his hand on his heart. 'I promise. So, what did your dad do after all of this? Did things change?'

Jody shook her head. 'No. He remembered my birthday that year, but that was it. I changed tack and started helping around The Bullion, hoping he'd notice me that way. But he didn't. In the end it was my art that saved me. I'd always doodled, but when I realised Dad was a lost cause I threw myself into it. I painted my sadness. Sculpted away my anger.'

'Your poor dad. He must've been completely heartbroken.'

A tide of anger rose up within Jody, but she quelled it. She knew that what Christian was saying was the truth. It was the conclusion she'd come to long ago. But hearing sympathy directed at her father was never easy, not when the ramifications of his heartbreak had been so great for his two children.

'It was his heart that gave out in the end, you know? The doctor put it down to drinking too much beer and eating the greasy pub food, but yeah... I think he'd struggled with the sadness long enough. At least he kept going until we were old enough and ugly enough to fend for ourselves.'

'And is that why you keep your life so insular? Just you and the boys? Because you want to ensure they never, not for one second, believe you aren't there for them?'

'It is. It's my job to keep their hearts safe.' *And mine.* A yawn escaped Jody's mouth. She clapped her hand over it, stopping it in its tracks. 'I'm sorry, it's been a long day. All that dancing.' *All those feelings...* 'Shall we go to bed?'

Christian's lips parted, shut, parted. 'Um... Are you sure?'

Oh God. He thought she meant go to bed as in *go to bed*. 'Oh!' she squeaked. 'No. Um. This is awkward. Not like that. I mean. You know. Separate beds. Me in mine. You in yours. Not in each other's. Not that you'd fit in mine. Single bed and all that...'

'Way to rescind an invitation.' Christian joked, but the humour in his tone didn't set his eyes sparkling. 'But yes, it's late. We have another big day ahead of us tomorrow. Bed sounds like the best option.'

'The sensible option,' Jody affirmed, as much to Christian as to herself.

Christian stood up and made his way inside and she followed suit, enjoying the view before her. The way his bottom filled out the back of his trousers, the way each cheek lifted and fell a little as he made his way up the stairs. The man had a very fine bum. It was such a pity she wouldn't get to see it naked...

166

CHAPTER TWELVE

Christian flipped from his side to his back, whipped the pillow from under his head and pushed it onto his face, letting out a frustrated groan. Why hadn't he stopped Jody from going to bed? He'd seen the indecision in her eyes as they'd said goodnight. She regretted telling him her story. That much was obvious. She was probably afraid his promising not to tell anyone meant nothing. She didn't know him. Didn't realise his whole life had been spent being the best he could be. And that included keeping the secrets of others. As far as his family's work and social circles knew, he came from a happy, successful, *normal* family. They had no idea of the emotional frigidity that lurked in his family home. A soul-deep shiver raced through him. He reached for the blankets and tucked them around himself, knowing no amount of material could warm the frostiness of his past.

Perhaps he should've stopped Jody from going to bed, sat her down and told her about his childhood, his past. About what it felt like to be an abject disappointment to your parents, despite doing your best, and in spite of being at the top of your game. Then they could've gone to bed, stories shared, troubles halved. Then perhaps rest would have come easy. Or not.

Christian shoved the pillow back under his head. His ears pricked up as a door in the house let out a long, high-pitched screech. Followed by floorboards creaking. Was it Jody? Was she up? Probably needed to go to the loo after all the wine and whiskey.

The quick tip-tap of feet passed the bathroom and stilled outside his door.

Three quiet taps followed. 'Christian? Are you awake?'

'Awake.' The word came out as a croak. Christian quietly cleared his throat. 'Come in.' He flicked on the bedside lamp, bathing the room in a soft golden glow.

The door swung open, revealing Jody, dressed in a grey T-shirt-style nightgown, her hair loose, feet bare, loitering at the door. Her gaze flicked around his room, uncertain, unsure. Then settled at her feet.

'Couldn't sleep?' he asked, trying to keep things light. Casual. With one foot in the bedroom, and the other out in the hallway, she looked ready to bolt.

'Something like that,' she whispered. Pink spots flushed high on her cheeks as the whisper of a smile played about her lips.

Christian ached to reach for her, to bring her into his embrace, to raise that terribly unsexy yet somehow alluring nightgown over her head, to lower his lips and taste her tanned shoulder, to explore every one of the hollows and hills surrounding her neck. Instinct told him to keep things cool, relaxed. She had to come to him or she'd regret it the next morning. And the last thing he wanted was for Jody to regret being with him, now, when she already regretted so many other actions in her life.

'Shall I warm you up some milk?' He made to get out of bed.

Jody reached his side in three strides. Her finger touched his lips. 'No, Christian. No milk. Also, no talking. Too much talking and I may scare myself off.'

Christian raised his hands in an attempt to hit pause on proceedings. 'Jody, I don't want you to scare yourself off. But I do want you to be sure.'

Jody saw Christian's hands go up and chose to ignore them. He was trying to be a gentleman, clearly. Trying to be decent, to let things happen slowly, romantically. She couldn't let him, though. She'd tried for calm, cool, collected, but it had been ten years.

Ten years was a long time to go without the touch of a man. She'd tried not to think about that fact while brushing her teeth, putting on her boring old nightgown and then tossing and turning for the last hour in her small single bed, but her lust-riddled head had done its darn best to make her aware of it. And for every reason it gave her to go to him, the minute amount of common sense she had left had put up an obstacle as to why she shouldn't.

Will you know what to do? Can you remember how to make a man moan? And how about that body? It's had two babies. Things aren't like they were when you were eighteen. Gravity, my friend, has taken its toll.

But despite all the reasons why going to Christian was a mistake, she'd found herself padding down the hallway…

'Jody…' Christian's hands were still held up, his fingers wide apart. She laced her fingers through his and closed them around his hands, ignoring whatever he wanted to say. If he stopped her now, she might not be able to continue.

'I just want to kiss you,' she whispered, and pressed herself into him, the only barrier between their bodies their interlaced hands, and far too much fabric. 'I just want to feel you against me.' Jody swallowed, and hoped he wouldn't be turned off by her honesty.

She released one hand and traced the ridges of his mouth, marvelled at how perfectly shaped his lips were, how strong. Made for kissing. Made for her. For one night only. That was the deal she'd made with herself when she had reached his bedroom door.

Her finger trailed down his chin and caressed his jawline. Sharp, strong, with a hint of stubble. She pushed him back against his pillow, climbed up on the bed, her knees at either side of his waist. Leaning over, she whispered into his ear. 'Just let me have you.'

'But…'

Jody's lips brushed against Christian's, silencing him.

'Don't stop me again,' she muttered against his mouth. 'There's nothing that can't wait.'

Christian hesitated, his gaze searching her face as if debating something, deciding something. But what?

He must have changed his mind, Jody realised. She'd come on too strong, turned him off, turned him away. She ignored the disappointment panging away in her heart. No matter. He was right. It was what she'd been telling herself all along… Falling for Christian, falling into bed with Christian, all of it was a bad idea. She gathered what little dignity she could muster and began to inch backwards away from Christian, away from face-flaming humiliation.

Christian's hand shot out and locked on to her hip, holding it lightly, stopping her in her tracks. Her head snapped up to see the indecision in Christian's eyes clear, replaced with resolve. And something hotter, primal.

He pulled her towards him, then reached up and clasped her head between his hands. His full mouth covering hers, kissing her, matching her fervour, as their tongues met, tasted. She fisted her hands in his hair, drove her tongue deeper. Harder. Her need for him building with every minute.

Jody broke the kiss. The time was now. No more interruptions. No more stalling. If things were going to go further, she needed to take the initiative. It was time he saw her. Post-baby body and all.

She straightened up in the bed, gathered the hem of the nightgown into her hands, gaining confidence as she saw Christian's eyes darken, his pupils dilating with desire. His eyes followed her progress as she lifted the hem higher and higher, tugging it over her head and tossing it to the ground, leaving her naked. Exposed.

It might have only been moments, seconds even, but to Jody the hot gaze of Christian taking her in, drinking her in, felt like an aeon. The longer he took, the louder her blood drummed in her ears, the harder her nerves rattled.

'Is it okay? Am I okay?' Her brief spark of confidence bolted for the hills. She crossed her arms over her body, wished there was a spare blanket on the bed so she could further hide herself.

'No.' The word came out as a growl as he pulled her down to him, tilting her chin so she was forced to look into his eyes. 'You are beautiful. Even more than I imagined. Every single part of you.' The words were dense with lust, yet clear with truth. 'Do you believe me?'

Jody went to nod but was stopped by Christian's lips once again meeting hers. One palm running up the spine of her back, the other encircling her waist, pulling her even closer, allowing her to feel how much he wanted her.

Her confidence renewed, Jody reached between them, found the waistband of Christian's pyjama bottoms and made to drag them down. 'I think since I'm in this state you ought to join me.' The molten heat, pooled down low, rushed up and over her cheeks, her renewed boldness taking her by surprise.

Christian chuckled, arched up and slipped off his pyjama bottoms, then in one fluid motion removed his T-shirt, revealing a model-hot muscular stomach. She'd kiss that stomach. Lick it. Commit it to memory. A work of art such as that deserved no less.

'We're still not on even footing...' Jody nodded in the direction of his underwear. Figure-hugging black boxer briefs, made even tauter by something sizeable and incredibly wantable straining at the fabric.

'Well, I was hoping you might do something about that for me.' Christian reached out and brought Jody back to him, holding her against him by her hips, hard enough she could feel his need for her, not so hard that she couldn't release it.

Her hands caressed the sides of his waist as she hooked her thumbs over his underwear and pushed it down, enjoying the view unfurling before her.

'Worth waiting for.' She breathed. Laughing a little as Christian helped her rip them off. Her amusement disappearing as he took control, his lips devouring, exploring, savouring. The room silent save for soft sighs, low moans, and whispered admirations, as they discovered each other, unable to be sated, oblivious to the hours that passed, the moon that began its descent, and the tide that flowed in, then began to roll out again.

* * *

A dip in temperature woke Jody. She scrambled around, eyes closed, looking for her blankets, only to hit something hard.

'Ow,' she muttered, half asleep. She went to glare at whatever the offending hand-hurter was, and to figure out where her blankets had disappeared to, but all she saw was Christian. Perfect, gorgeous, sexy Christian. He lay beside her, one hand cupping his head, his other arm tucked around his pillow. The blanket she'd been searching for twisted around his legs. His face was still, bar for a wrinkle between his eyes that deepened at irregular intervals. Was he having a bad dream? Jody hoped not. Not after their night together. No nightmare would dare ruin what had been an unforgettable night.

And it had been truly unforgettable. Passionate, tender, hot, sensual. A night unlike any other she'd experienced, or perhaps would again. From may-as-well-have-been-a-virgin to vixen, then back to born-again-virgin in less than twenty-four hours.

One night. That was her plan. And she had to stick to it. For her. For the boys. For their family.

She scanned the darkened room for another blanket, but with none in sight she fended off the chill by curling up and around Christian, breathing in his scent. Allowing herself one last moment of taking him in before the day would begin, and her night of pleasure would be over.

Over? You couldn't stop yourself from going back if you tried.

Jody tried to fight the voice of reason, of truth. Of course she could resist Christian. Once was more than enough. She'd gone a decade without feeling the pull of temptation, so she could go another, and even if she did feel her resistance lowering, it wasn't like she would be faced with that temptation. There would be no bumping into Christian at the shops, in the pub, at the café. No, he'd be going back to his life in London soon enough. And she'd be at home in Rabbits Leap, alone with her boys.

As if sensing her plans to back off, Christian abandoned cuddling his pillow and wrapped his arm around her, bringing her closer. His lips pressed against the back of her head.

'Morning,' he murmured.

'Morning?' Jody whispered. 'Is it morning? It's so dark?'

'Blackout curtains,' Christian replied, sliding his hand across her belly, down her waist, over her hip, further down, before pausing.

Jody hesitated, torn between taking things further and being up, awake, and moving towards her renewed singledom. If she said yes to what he was silently asking for, she'd be breaking her latest promise of 'never again' in one minute flat. If she said no, she'd be ignoring the want pulsing through her veins.

She nuzzled further into him, thanking the owner of the flat for installing blackout curtains. She could pretend it was still night. Pretend this was an extension of the one night only.

She could pretend for a few more hours that once with Christian would be enough.

CHAPTER THIRTEEN

'You've been quiet today.' Christian glanced sideways at Jody, sitting ramrod straight in her seat as they made their way back to Rabbits Leap. Her eyes focused on the road. Her hands clasped in her lap. Every inch of her might as well have been wearing a 'keep out' sign.

'I'm just tired. It's been a tiring trip.' She stifled a yawn that, to Christian, looked very much fake.

'We only have ourselves to blame for that.' Christian tried for a joke but it fell as flat as Jody's energy. If he wanted her to engage with him he'd have to change tack. 'Good the jazz band's signed up. They'll make for some great morning entertainment. I spoke to Mrs Harper earlier today too. Turns out my contact at the regional paper printed a story about the festival, and it's struck a chord with people. The tickets have sold out and we've had dozens of requests from people wanting to pay for stall space. The festival's getting bigger by the day. We just need to figure out where to fit them. Do you think Tony would let us clear out the dining area of The Bullion? We could put some tables in there…'

'That's great. Really great.' Jody crossed one leg over the other.

Away from him, Christian noted as he fought back an exasperated sigh, and failed. 'You're not listening to a word I say. And your body language is distinctly saying it doesn't want to be in the same space as me. I don't understand what's going on, Jody. Should I have made you two cups of tea this morning? Was buying you bacon and eggs for brunch not enough? Should I have added a side of "apology", because I feel like you're pissed off at me and I don't know what I've done to deserve it.'

Jody's nose straightened as her nostrils flared. 'Nothing.' The word was tight, tense. 'And that's the problem. You've done nothing to help me get over you. Can't you go and be a dick or something so I can dislike you?'

'What?' Christian pulled the car over to the verge without bothering to indicate, ignoring the angry beep from the car behind him. 'Why would you be trying to get over me? We've only just begun—'

'No. That's the thing. There's nothing to begin. There can't be. Don't you get that, Christian?' Jody faced him, fire burning in her eyes. 'Even if I was in the market for a relationship, which I'm not, it would have to be with someone who was going to stick around. Christian, you're not going to stick around Rabbits

178

Leap. You couldn't. You're used to the rat-race pace, and sure, you're enjoying a breather here in Rabbits Leap, but you'll get bored. You'll tire of going at a trot instead of a gallop. And where would that leave me? And the boys? Because you have to realise I'm a package deal, Christian. I said exactly that when we first met.'

'But...' Christian trailed off. He knew she had a point, that he would have to go back to London. He'd have to face the music for his mistake at some point. To go into damage control. But he hadn't wanted to think further than the here and now, because for the first time in a long time he was having a properly good time. He'd loved discovering the secret corners and incredible surprises that every conversation, every interaction, with Jody brought. He'd enjoyed spending time with the boys, getting to know their quirks. Sure they were identical but their personalities gave them separate identities. Tyler with his slight sneers whenever he thought something was stupid. Jordan with the little mole on his cheek that disappeared into his dimple when he smiled, which was freely and often. The way the boys looked at him, how they held his hands so trustingly... it made him feel like there was more to life. That there could be more to *his* life.

'You see my point, don't you?' Jody pursed her lips as if the matter were settled. But it wasn't, not by a long shot. Christian had believed himself to be successful. A great career. A nice home. Friends

179

with the right people. But now he'd discovered success meant warm smiles across glasses of wine and lemonade, small hands tugging on his shirt when attention was required, lingering kisses that held so much promise. He wasn't letting that go so easily. He wasn't giving up without a fight.

'No. I don't see your point. Not at all.' Christian reached for Jody's hand but she tugged it away and tucked it under her thigh. 'What I see is a woman who is afraid to open her heart to anyone. Sure, you love your boys, of course you do, you're their mother. And they adore you. But you won't let anyone else in. And I can't help but think it's because of the way you grew up, with love taken away from you. First, when your mother passed away. Second, when your father's heart broke. And then when you thought you could spend your life with the boys' father.'

'That's not true,' Jody protested in a strangled whisper. 'I loved my grandparents. And I love Tony.'

'But they were around from the start. Who have you let into your life, into your heart, that wasn't there right from the beginning?'

The silence between then stretched out, filling the air with almost unbearable tension.

Christian shook his head as he turned from Jody. 'You know, you're not the only one who's struggled with family. With relationships. Do you know my parents haven't spoken to me in nearly fifteen years? They wanted me to follow them down the medicine or lawyer path. Respectable jobs. Jobs that mattered. Jobs like theirs. The pressure was there from the time I started school. Perhaps even before. Anything less than top marks was treated with disdain. Hell, top marks weren't even congratulated. They were expected. But as much as I tried, I couldn't reach their expectations. I chose to do a law degree. Worked hard. Studied all night. But my heart wasn't in it, and it showed in my marks.' Christian glanced over at Jody whose face was firmly forward. Was she hearing a word he was saying? There was only one way to find out. He had to let it all out. 'Around that time a friend was planning a birthday party. A big affair, with DJs and bands, on his family's estate in Suffolk. I offered to help out and discovered I was good at organising and directing others. The party was huge. Massive. It spurred me on to do something I'd never done before. I displeased my parents and followed my heart. I quit the law degree and instead studied event management. Got top marks too, not that they cared.' A humourless snort filled the air. 'During the nights I worked my arse off as a casual for an event management organisation. Garnered the respect of my boss, who offered me a job once my degree was done. I climbed the ranks. I'd email my parents links to articles featuring the events. Even though I should've known better, I was still trying to show them I was worthy of their attention, of their love. They never emailed back. As far as they were concerned I was a letdown to the family name. Slowly but surely they froze me out, which only made me work harder. Be better. To show them they were wrong. It also taught me to keep people who could hurt me at a distance. My relationships were superficial. Hell, even my friends don't know that much about me. I've never let them close enough. In following my heart, I lost it. But I'm willing to follow it again, Jody. Because I think we could have something special together, if you'd only give it a chance.'

He waited for a response. None was forthcoming. He started up the car and pulled out onto the road. He should've known better than to hope his life could change. Even if he wanted to be with Jody, she didn't want the same. It was like he'd found the one person who'd turn him down, turn him away. A fresh way of showing himself he'd never be good enough for those whose attention he wanted most.

'How would our life be if I were to give us a chance? Would I move to London with the boys, upset their routine, their lives? Would you give up everything you've worked for to settle in a small village where there's one festival a year, the Farmer of the Year Awards and a Christmas parade to keep you busy. That wouldn't be enough for someone like you.'

'London isn't that far away.' Renewed hope filled Christian with cautious joy. 'We could take things slowly. I could come down whenever I didn't have to be on site for an event. Work from Rabbits Leap as much as possible. I'd stay at The Bullion. That way, if you were to decide it was too hard, that things between us were never going to work, it wouldn't impact the boys too greatly. They'd remember me as their mother's friend, no more. But if things worked out? When you were ready, I'd leave London to be with you.'

Jody chewed on her lower lip. What was happening? How was this happening? Was there a way to get out of it? Did she even want to? Was it about want or need? She needed to keep herself safe from hurt. She had to be strong for the boys. Had to be there for them. Had to be the opposite of her father.

'I'm sorry, Christian. I am. I don't see how it could work. You'd get bored of our quiet little life. You'd need the excitement, the adrenaline rush of success. I saw how you were last night when you signed the band. You live for that. I can't take it away from you. I won't.'

Christian's face fell. All hope drained from his eyes. She felt like a right evil cow, but she needed time. To process. From one night to being offered the chance of a proper relationship in a few short hours? It was too much. Too fast.

Or perhaps she was just too scared.

'Jody, no. I'm sorry, but you're wrong. You've made me see there's another way to live. A more solid way. With substance. Quiet coffees at Mel's. Meanders through fields. Leisurely lunches at Tony's. My life has been hollow. Rabbits Leap has filled a good chunk of that emptiness. But most of it's been filled by you. And the boys. How can you not see that?'

Jody's head jerked back at the bitterness in Christian's voice. He must think her horrible. She couldn't blame him. Her gut roiled with self-loathing. He'd put his heart out for her and she'd trampled all over it. But she couldn't worry about his heart when hers was on the line.

Christian turned the car into the tight and windy hedgerow-enclosed lane that led to Rabbits Leap, only to be forced to slow the car down to a halt. The bleating of sheep filled the air.

'Really,' he muttered, his brows furrowed together in frustration.

'I'm sorry, Christian.' The words came out a whisper.

'No. I'm sorry. I'm sorry you can't see that you're just like your father. He blocked you from his heart to save his own. That much is obvious. And you're following suit. Blocking me to save yourself. It's funny how we so often become like the people we least want to be like. Me, a workaholic like my parents with no real emotional connections to anyone. You, a person who refuses to entertain emotional connections with anyone who might leave. The boys are fine. Tony is fine. They're part of you. But me? I could leave and you can't risk that. I get that. But you should risk it, or you could end up very lonely one day. And I'd hate to see that.'

Jody clapped her hands over her ears. She didn't want to know she was like her father. Didn't want to

184

believe it. But the churning in her stomach was telling her otherwise. Telling her Christian was right. How had it come to this? How had she turned into the person she so wanted to be nothing like? Another wave of nausea rolled through her. She thrust open the door, leant out and released the contents of her stomach. She heaved and heaved until all that was left was a thin line of spittle reaching from her mouth to the ground. Her self-loathing had grown to self-hatred and no amount of chundering was going to expel those feelings. She'd have to face them.

She blinked and wiped away the tears in her eyes, then swiped her hand over her mouth.

'Are you okay?'

The light pressure of Christian's hand on her upper arm brought her to her senses.

'No. I'm not okay.' She straightened up, her back against the seat and watched as masses of sheep were mustered from one field to the next. Sheepdogs barking in the distance told Jody she and Christian were going to be stuck together in the car for some time yet. She cursed quietly to herself.

'I've never heard you say that word.' Christian's fingers tapped the steering wheel to an invisible tune.

'I save it for when it's really needed.' Jody massaged her temples as a headache began to burrow its way into her head.

'Yes, I can imagine how this situation would warrant that word. Having a man tell you he thinks you're amazing, having him want to be part of your life, it must be a real drain.' The tapping stopped. He gripped the steering wheel, white knuckles strained against the skin.

Jody groaned as a stab of pain arrowed its way through her brain.

'Sorry to state the obvious.' Christian didn't sound sorry at all.

'It's not you,' Jody murmured, not wanting to raise her voice in case it caused another arrow of agony. 'It's me. And I'm not saying that as a way to make this situation better. I mean, you've already figured out it's not you, it's me. You know.'

'Uh-huh,' Christian snorted.

'I never wanted to be like him. Had pretty much convinced myself I wasn't. I mean, I love the boys so much. Probably too much. Good old-fashioned overcompensation and all that. But I had to love them that much. It was the only way to erase the feelings I had late at night when I'd wonder what my life would have been like without them. I was all set to go to City & Guilds, you know? I was on my way to achieving the first of many dreams I'd made for myself. Get out of Rabbits Leap. Go to art school. Travel round Europe seeking inspiration. Then creating works that inspired others. That was the plan.'

'And then the unplanned pregnancy...' Christian's hands released their firm grip on the wheel.

'Exactly. The plan changed. I was stuck in Rabbits Leap with two little humans totally dependent on me.

Dreams dashed. But it's not a bad life. Helping with the festival has reminded me of how special Rabbits Leap is. Where else has a marsh spirit with a warped sense of humour?' She attempted a smile, but it quickly faded.

'It is a special place. With very special people. One of those people is sitting next to me. I just hope she knows how special she is. And you know what, Jody. You'll get your dreams. We'll find a way...'

Christian's voice was as earnest as it was determined. Two damp patches from her tears formed on Jody's knees and trickled down her legs.

She angled her head to face Christian. 'How can you be so nice to me after I've been a complete cow to you?'

'It's surprising what you'll do for someone you have big and scary grown-up feelings for.' Christian's finger stroked the side of her cheek, taking another tear with it.

'Funny. You're kind to me. I behave like an absolute horror to you.'

'If that's how you show your big and scary grown-up feelings, then I guess I'll have to get used to it.' Christian's eyes crinkled at the edges as he caressed her hair. 'The question is, where do we go from here?'

Jody massaged her temples. How had one night of fun evolved into one moment where she could choose to stay the path, to doggedly hold on to old hang-ups, or change her life? Change herself. But could she?

Christian was saying all the right words, doing all the right things, but did that equate to his being the right man?

'I don't know I'm girlfriend material...' She rolled the word round in her mouth, then released it once more. 'Girlfriend. It's not the worst word in the world, is it?'

'Sounds good from where I'm sitting.'

Jody dropped her hands into her lap and took in the sheep leisurely trailing past. It came down to one thing. Would not giving Christian a chance lead to her having one more thing to regret?

'Could we take things slower than slow? Snail's pace?' A sliver of elation arrowed through the fear of rejection that had held her heart hostage for so many years. If she dipped a toe in, then sank in bit by bit, maybe she could give this relationship business a chance.

'We can take things however you want them, Jody. I won't push. I only ask you to give it a proper go, and if you find yourself freaking out, don't hold it in. Talk it through with me. Give us the chance to work it out together.'

Jody took hold of Christian's hand, brought it to her lips and kissed his palm. 'I'm not going to be my father. I won't. So let's do this. Let's give us a go.' She blew out a shaky breath. 'Oh, these big, grown-up feelings are hard.'

A wolf-whistle sliced through the air as a grinning farmer peered in at the two of them, making kissy motions and doing a silly dance.

'I can't believe I'm prepared to move here.' Christian shook his head in wonder. 'I must be completely bonkers.'

Jody shooed the farmer off after his flock. 'I'm not going to disagree with you.'

***

'Jody. Wake up.'

Jody opened her eyes, then shut them again as the sun threatened to blind her. Where were they? She half-opened one eye to see the street she knew as well as the back of her hand. The Bullion's doors were open wide and she could see people sitting at the bar enjoying Tony's brews. The butcher's sign swung idly in the breeze. Fairy lights danced around Mel's Café. The recently weeded, thanks to Christian's direction, flowerboxes brimmed with colour. A few local kids were sliding down the rabbit in the park.

How had she ever thought she didn't want to live here? How had she ever believed there could be a place better than home?

'You awake, sleepyhead?'

She turned to Christian and smiled. Perhaps what she'd been waiting for was for her heart to find a place to call home, and perhaps, just maybe, it had found a home in the man sitting beside her. 'I'm awake.'

'Shall we go see the boys?' He unbuckled his seatbelt and swung the door open.

We. The word warmed her soul. It seemed Christian really was serious about her, about the boys. He could've gone straight back to his room at The Bullion, but instead he wanted to spend time with them.

The passenger door opened and Christian held his hand out to her. Jody slid her feet into her sandals, took his hand and let him help her out. She took a moment to stretch out her arms and legs, the muscles bunched up after the long ride home.

'You look like you're stalling. Are you stalling?' Christian squeezed her hand.

'No. Maybe,' she admitted. 'It's just... What if the boys are freaked out about their mum liking someone else? What if they get angry? What if their opinion matters so much to me that it means there won't be any us?' She bit her lip and shifted from foot to foot. She didn't want to hurt Christian, but she had to prepare him for her biggest 'what if?' fear coming true.

The tinkle of Mel's coffee shop's doorbell alerted Jody to the presence of another person.

'Serena! Look at that! Mum's holding Christian's hand!' Jordan ran towards them, with Tyler close on his heels.

'Well, I guess we're about to find out what the boys think...' Christian murmured into her hair, before giving it a quick kiss.

'And Christian just kissed Mum's head,' Tyler exclaimed, sliding into the back of his brother with an 'oof'.

'Are you sick, Mum?' Tyler took her other hand. 'Can I feel your head?'

'Mum always kisses our heads when we're sick,' Jordan explained to Christian.

'Doesn't hold our hands when we're being sick. She rubs our back, though. Soooo…' Jordan's eyes widened as if he'd been hit with a life-changing thought. 'If Mum's not sick and you're holding hands, and you just kissed her, Christian, does that mean you're her boyfriend?'

Jody rolled her eyes. 'Jordan, if the police ever need a detective I'm going to send you their way.'

'Does that mean he's right, Mum?' Tyler asked, a little line running between his eyebrows.

'It means Christian and I are good friends.'

'Oh.' The line disappeared. 'Well, if you want to be more than good friends it would be okay with us. We had a team talk.'

'A team talk?' Jody squatted down to Tyler and Jordan's level, then bobbed back up a bit. They were getting taller, she realised. More mature. They weren't the young boys she still had in her mind's eye. 'What's a team talk?'

'It's when friends and family get together to talk about things of importance. That's what Uncle Tony said. So he, me, Jordan and Aunty Mel talked about you. And we decided you needed more than us two boys. We suggested we could get you a pet, but Uncle Tony said you needed something that could talk.'

'Yeah, so we came up with Christian. You talk to him. He talks to you. And you didn't hit him in the nuts right now when he held your hand. So you must like each other.'

'Out of the mouths of babes,' Christian murmured.

'We're not babes.' Jordan stomped his foot. 'We're boys.'

'Too right you are.' Christian mussed up Jordan's hair. 'Now, who could go for an ice cream?'

'Me!' the boys yelled in unison, before grabbing Christian by his hands and dragging him up to the shops.

'So, good business trip, huh?' Serena sidled up to Jody and nudged her with her hip.

'You might say that.' Jody winked at her friend, dressed in the usual Serena-style – a vermillion off-the-shoulder crop top with ruffles across the chest and a pair of glittery gold hot pants. Bright, brilliant, flouncy, and more suited to some glamorous seaside party resort than a quiet farming village. Jody wondered how long Serena would stay before excitement came calling again.

'You're all sorted then?' Serena dipped her chin and raised her eyebrows.

Jody knew exactly what she was getting at. 'Yep, got the two bands for the festival sorted.' She kept her face straight as Serena's flushed the same colour as her top.

'Seriously? Really? Is that all you're going to tell your oldest friend? Your best friend?' Serena stomped her foot in a similar manner to Jordan's seconds before. 'Look, I'm gagging for gossip over here. Not just any gossip. Yours. Tell me all the dirty details.'

'I spewed on the way home. Is that dirty enough for you?'

Serena clapped a hand over her mouth, then let it slide slowly down to her chin. 'No way? Does this mean you're pregnant again? Can morning sickness strike that quickly?'

'You really know that little about babies and baby making?'

Serena shrugged, apparently unperturbed. 'I'm an only child. I left Rabbits Leap before you had your kidlets. And considering my lack of someone to make a baby with, I'm not about to have any myself. There's no reason for me to know any of the itty-bitty details.'

'But you do know the basics, right?' Jody teased.

Serena tossed her long black curls over her shoulder and laughed. 'You put your winky in, you put your winky out...' she sang along to the tune of the 'Hokey Cokey'.

Jody put her hand up, silencing her friend. 'Yeah, yeah. I know you know, you don't have to be a smartarse about it.'

'So what was with the puking?' Serena interlocked her fingers behind her back and stretched, letting out a soft groan. 'Eat something bad?'

'No, just let everything get on top of me. You know how it is. One moment you're sailing along in a boring but safe routine. Next thing you know…'

'You meet a man when you've sworn you won't. You fall head over heels in love and the realisation of that makes you sick to your stomach?'

'I'm not in love.' Jody wrapped her arms around her chest and shook her head. 'I'm in…like.'

'You're not the person to just do "like", Jody McArthur.' Serena gently unwrapped Jody's hands and took them in her own. 'You've too big a heart. I may not have been around much in the last twelve or so years, but I know you well enough to know you could have been courted by any number of men about these parts. You're beautiful, talented, funny. They'd be lucky to have you. But you've stayed single as you promised yourself you would. So, for you to be holding hands with a man, it must mean you've decided one night wasn't enough.'

Jody closed her eyes to the words, but she couldn't close her ears, or her heart. Even though Christian had been a total arse at their first meeting, his assertion of what would work for the festival had been because he wanted the best for the town. And because failure wasn't an option for him or his career. Now, though? He was willing to move here to be with her. That would no doubt impact his career in a major way. But he didn't care. Because he cared about her, and the boys.

'Are you all right in there?' Jody's hands were given a light shake. 'Am I going to have to tickle you to get you to come out?' There was concern in Serena's voice.

Jody opened her eyes. 'No. You don't have to tickle me. But if this all goes wrong, will you promise to help me pick up the pieces of my heart?'

'I'll bring the shovel and brush. But I hope I won't have to. But if he hurts you...'

'You'll sic that crazy cow of yours on him?'

'You know it. Daisy packs a mean fart.' Serena pulled Jody into a hug.

'Mum!' A delighted Jordan trotted up to them, his chin covered in a wet-looking white beard. 'Look at the size of this ice cream! Christian bought us the biggest ones they had!'

'Very generous of him,' Jody replied drily. 'You'd better eat your dinner after this. And you'd better too...' Jody nodded at Christian, who was walking up to them hand in hand with Tyler. Both licking their way through humongous ice creams.

'And if I don't?' Christian arched an eyebrow.

'You won't get dessert,' Jody replied with a wink.

'But he's already got dessert, Mum.' Tyler looked up at Jody as if she'd lost her marbles, causing Serena's raucous laugh to rumble about the main street.

'And on that note,' she said, 'I've got cows to milk. I'll catch you later.' She turned to Christian. 'And you be good to her, or else.' She waggled her index finger in warning.

Jody watched her friend jump in the pick-up truck, rev the engine and pull out into the street in a flurry of waving hand. Jody matched her friend's grin as she raced by, yelling 'enjoy dessert!' out the window.

'So, shall we head home?' Christian asked. An innocent enough question, but it created a knot in Jody's stomach. Home had always been her and the boys. Would home really have room for one more?

CHAPTER FOURTEEN

Christian took in the small cottage that was Jody's haven away from the world. It was the complete opposite of his spacious flat in London, with its open-plan living, crisp white walls, bare save for a few abstract paintings, blonde polished wooden floorboards, top-of-the-line kitchen appliances in his small kitchen, and the intrusion of a bustling city spilling in whenever he opened the windows.

A world away, yet it suited her and the boys perfectly, and the moment he'd entered he'd felt comfortable. Almost like part of the furniture. Which wasn't hard to believe as the boys were treating him very much like a piece of furniture, climbing all over him, leaping off his shoulders, getting him to act as a vertical plank they could climb up while holding his hands, before flipping themselves over and landing back on the ground.

'Tyler. Jordan. Give Christian a break. He's only just got here. Christian, cup of tea?'

'Yes, please.' Christian gave her the thumbs-up as the boys launched another assault on his back.

Jody gave him a weak smile and walked through to the kitchen.

Was it his imagination or was Jody acting a little... off? During the drive home she'd been distant. Answering questions in a monosyllabic fashion. Interacting with the boys only when they asked a question. For the most part she'd turned her head towards the window, and Christian suspected if he asked her what she'd seen on the way home the answer would be 'nothing much', despite his witnessing the building of an eight-feet-tall scarecrow, two locals running around their front yard, one brandishing a rolled-up newspaper at the other, who was nude save for a cushion covering his privates, and a pheasant eyeing up the car in a way that had made Christian slow down in case it was tempted to jump from the rock wall it was perched on onto the car's windscreen.

'Boys, can I chat to your mum for a minute?' Christian disentangled himself, ignoring their groans of disappointment and stepped into the cosy kitchen. 'God, you mustn't want to leave this room come winter. I bet that potbelly keeps everything nice and toasty.' He pulled out one of the fifties-style chrome and vinyl dining chairs, sat down and tapped his fingers rhythmically on the matching mottled-turquoise formica table. Anything to break the silence coming from Jody's direction. 'So, what do you have planned for the rest of the day?' he asked, hoping an open-ended question would get more than a few words out of her.

Jody spooned sugar into the mugs and added a teabag to each. 'I was thinking I'd send the boys outside to play and try to do a little painting. I'm in a painting kind of mood.' Jody poured hot water from the kettle into the mugs.

'Is that what's making you so quiet? You said you used painting and sculpting to help you with your feelings. Are you having some of those big, grown-up feelings we talked about right now? Because of me? Us? Or something else?' Christian had a feeling he already knew the answer, but wanted to hear it from Jody's mouth. Better to keep the line of communication open and clear than to dwell in murkiness.

Jody removed the teabags from the mugs and plopped them into the sink, then swirled in some milk and sat Christian's mug on the table, before picking up her own and blowing into it to cool it down. 'You know, this not being like my father is harder than I expected. It's like I want to say something and it gets clamped down before the words come out. And then, to further justify my position, I come up with all these reasons in my head as to why you and I won't work. The latest being that it's all going a little faster than I expected and I'm feeling scared,' she said, taking a sip of her tea. 'There, I said it. Got it out. I guess I'm not completely shut down after all.'

'I'm not sure what you mean?' Christian wrapped his hand around the mug, the sting of heat helping him to focus. 'I don't know why you'd feel scared. I said we could do long-distance. And we wouldn't race into anything until you're absolutely sure about us.' Maybe that was what was causing the strain between them. Maybe Jody was sure, and it scared her? 'Look, I don't want to pressure you into anything and I appreciate that painting will help you clear your head. How about...' He spun the mug around lazily. 'How about I take the boys out for the rest of the afternoon? I'm sure the farmer with the ponies we're hiring for the festival wouldn't mind if we paid him a visit and tested them out.'

Jody set the mug down and crossed her arms over her chest. 'I'm not sure the boys would be into it. I mean, they've only spent time with you when I was with them. They might find it a bit weird if I'm not there...'

'Is that you finding excuses again? You did see the boys clambering over me just now, right? I think the boys are fine in my company. Please don't use them as some kind of human emotion blockade.' Christian kept his tone measured, but his heart began to thump against his chest. He wasn't going to let this relationship fail before it had even started.

'Is this what life with you is going to be like?' Jody picked up her tea and paused at the door. 'You're always going to pull me up when I'm just trying to protect myself?' She turned her back on him and left.

Christian followed the sound of her footsteps and found her trudging up the stairs. 'Yes. It's exactly what I'm going to do. I refuse to accept failure as an option – it's probably the best trait my parents gave me.

So, whenever that brain of yours tries to scare itself back into its emotion cave, I'm going to tease, pull and, if I have to, yank you back into the real world.'

He stepped into a small room, covered in canvasses. Images of Rabbits Leap surrounded him. The pub in a derelict state, a shadow cast over it. The rape fields in full bloom, the brilliant blue of the sky a stunning contrast. On the table in the middle of the room was a large swathe of fabric, on which Jody was currently painting. 'Is that the festival sign? It looks brilliant.' And it did. Hundreds of rabbits ran along the bottom of the fabric, climbing up and over the letters. To either side musicians played their instruments. A representation of the Rabbit Revolt. 'You're so talented. I love the picture of the pub.'

'That was my first painting I worked on after I'd trashed the pool. It represents the shadow that fell over my conscience.'

'And the rape fields?'

'I was heavily pregnant. Blooming as they bloomed.'

'We should include an art show at the festival. We could put your work out there. Make inroads on one of those dreams of yours. Maybe make enough money to get you to Europe.'

Jody shook her head and went back to painting the sign. 'No, I don't think so. I wouldn't want to use the festival as a way of earning money when I'm doing it to apologise for my actions. It wouldn't feel right. If the town ever found out the truth about what I did, they'd see it as selfish, as using them for my own ends.'

Christian stood beside Jody and placed a hand on her shoulder, turning her towards him. 'You know, you could just admit to it, Jody. I'm sure they'd forgive you. You're loved in this town.'

'Just leave it alone, Christian. Please.' She shrugged his hand off and went back to work. 'I'm doing it my way. It might not be the best way, but it's the only way I can think of that won't impact the boys. If the town knew, they could be teased by the other kids. The boys may even see me differently. I'd hate that. I've worked too hard to make sure there's no reason for them not to love me.'

'Those boys couldn't not love you if they tried. You're their world and nothing can change that.'

Jody ignored his words, instead bending closer to the painting, apparently absorbed in some finer detail.

'Fine. You be like that. But I'm going to tell you straight, Jody. This lack of communication, this switching off when you don't like the territory... You know as well as I do that's what you've learnt from your father. Don't be like him, Jody. Be you.'

He waited for a reply. None came. 'Fine. Just think about what I've said. Think about who you want to be. I'll take the boys out, get them out of your hair while you do this.'

Jody looked up. 'Make sure you bring them home in one piece, Christian. They're my world.'

Christian exhaled his frustration, spun on his heel and went outside to round up the boys. *They*. Not *you*.

Would he ever be good enough for someone he cared about?

**

'Those boys sure are having a good time,' Mr Sturridge observed as the boys circled the field for what felt like the millionth time, wide toothy grins lighting up their faces.

'Yeah. They're good horses you've got there. Patient. I'm surprised they're not getting spooked with all that hooting and hollering.'

'Well, they've done a few shows. They're used to the noise.'

'And you've never had an incident?' Christian sank down onto the lush grass. All this standing alert had been tiring work, but the boys were doing as they were told. Holding on to the reins with both hands, not playing silly buggers. It wouldn't hurt to take a load off. He tipped his head towards the late-afternoon sun and closed his eyes, allowing the warmth to bathe his face.

'Jordan, stop being a dick!' Tyler yelled at his brother.

Christian's eyes snapped open. What was happening? Was Tyler okay? What had he been thinking, taking two seconds to relax? Was he an idiot? Jody had made it quite clear he was to keep a close eye on them, and he'd slacked off. The last time he'd slacked off, one of the world's most beloved singers had very nearly died. 'Boys, what's going on over there?' He sprang up to see Jordan keeping pace with Tyler, reaching over and trying to poke his brother in the waist. 'Jordan, if you want to come down from that pony, then you'll keep doing what you're doing. If you want to continue having a fun afternoon, then by all means cut that behaviour out. Right. Now.'

Jordan swung to face Christian, his eyes flat. 'You're not the boss of me.' Without breaking eye contact, he leaned over and poked Tyler again. Tyler held on to the reins, but tipped dangerously to one side.

'Jordan. I'm not joking around. Get back here with that pony now.'

'And if I don't?' Jordan made to nudge his brother, who'd only just managed to right himself, again.

'What do you think your mother would say if anything happened to you or your brother? Do you think we'd be allowed to have pony rides at the festival?'

Jordan didn't budge. *Shit.* He was going to have to bring out the big guns.

'Do you think she'd ever let me take you out for ice cream ever again?' Christian held his breath and hoped the ice cream threat would work.

Jordan nudged the pony in its sides and started to walk over to Christian.

Thank God. Christian exhaled long and slow. For a second there he'd had images of Tyler falling off the pony, of his head being trampled, and selfishly, of any

204

hope of future happiness disappearing in a puff of sun-dried dust.

'Woah, boy.' Mr Sturridge patted the pony's neck as it came to a stop. 'You good to get down from there, son?' he asked Jordan.

'Sure,' Jordan replied sullenly.

Christian held his hand out for Jordan to grab if he needed it, but Jordan screwed up his nose. 'I'm not useless, you know,' Jordan muttered, taking one foot out of the stirrup and swinging it round the hind of the horse.

Christian's heart slammed against his ribcage as Jordan overbalanced and began to fall off the horse, his left leg still positioned in the stirrup. He leapt forward to try and catch him, his stomach going into free-fall as Jordan's body hit the ground with a soft thunk, a cry piercing the air.

Was that cry from him? Tyler, who was trotting towards them? Or Jordan, whose eyes were wide, his face ashen, his left foot still in the stirrup, the ankle swelling up before his eyes?

'We need a doctor. Where's the doctor. Mr Sturridge? Can you call a doctor to come?'

'There, there, boy,' Mr Sturridge soothed, gently removing the stirrup from Jordan's foot and placing his leg gently on the ground. 'There, there.'

Christian knelt beside Jordan and stroked his hair away from his face. 'Jordan? Are you okay?'

'Can I say a swear word?' Jordan asked, his eyes welling with tears.

'Just this once. I won't tell,' Christian promised, hope easing the pounding of his heart. If Jordan could talk, then things couldn't be too bad.

'This bloody…' Jordan's eyes rolled back in his head. He went silent.

Hope died as panic set in. 'Mr Sturridge. We need an ambulance. Now.'

'No ambulances around here, lad. At least not for a sprain. The doctor's probably at the pub by now, so we could pack the young fellow up into your car and head that way.'

'That's not what I wanted to hear,' he said through gritted teeth.

A moan escaped Jordan's lips as he began to come round. 'Mum?' he whispered. 'I want Mum.'

'We'll get her, Jordan.' Christian gripped his hand and attempted a reassuring smile. 'We'll get you sorted too. We're just going to have to carry you to the car. It might hurt. Can you be brave?'

'What choice does he have?' Mr Sturridge asked as he scooped the boy up and strode towards the car. 'Also, I'm driving. You look like you're about to pass out yourself.'

***

Jody raced into The Bullion, not caring that her car was parked in the middle of the street, the keys dangling in the ignition, the door flung wide open. Some person on the make could steal her car and never

206

bring it back for all she cared. All she wanted was to get to her son.

'Jordan? Jordan!' she called, not knowing why she was yelling when it was obvious from the crowd milling about the bar where the boys were. She elbowed her way through the rubberneckers, and reached the bar to find Jordan sitting on it, a glass of lemonade in his hand, his foot propped up by a couple of cushions. Christian pacing back and forth. Tyler nowhere to be found.

'What the hell is going on here?' she demanded as she reached Jordan's side and grabbed his hand. 'Jordan, are you okay?' Not waiting for an answer she rounded on Christian, grabbing him by his wrist and stopping him in mid pace. 'What did I say to you! I told you to look after them. This isn't what looking after them looks like.'

'Mum, it wasn't his—'

'No.' Jody cut Jordan short. 'I want to hear it from Christian.'

'God, I'm so sorry, Jody. So sorry. I can't believe this has happened. Again. And I was watching. I was. Every second. Didn't take my eyes off them. Well, maybe for one second. Stupid,' he muttered. 'But he's okay. That's the main thing. It's not serious. Not like the last time.'

Blood roared in Jody's ears. Had she just heard that right? Again? What else had this man she'd been so close to letting in done? 'Did I just hear you right? You said "again". What else have you done? And why don't I know about it? All this talk of communication and you've been keeping something from me.'

'It's not a big deal, Jody.' Christian resumed his pacing. 'I mean, it was. A woman nearly died. But she didn't. And she's fine. Madam Foxy survived. My career may not, but that's not really what matters right now. It's Jordan. And he is okay. He'll be sore, but he'll be fine.' Christian stopped and reached out to Jody.

She took a step back. She didn't want him to touch her. Didn't want him anywhere near her. Not after this. 'Madam Foxy. The pop singer who nearly died after being fed something she was allergic to? That was you?' She hugged her arms tight around her chest and tried to stem the angry tears that were threatening to flow. 'God, I'm such an idiot. I knew you being here was too good to be true. What were you doing? Hiding out? Never mind, I don't care. God, I can't believe I trusted you with the boys.' Jody seethed, as angry at Christian as she was with herself. 'I can't believe I trusted you at all. If I'd known you were the cause of Madam Foxy's near-death experience I wouldn't have touched you with a barge pole. I'm a fool. I should never have hired you to help me fix the damn festival. I shouldn't have wasted my money!' Jody slapped her hand over her mouth. What had she just said? Out loud? In the pin-drop-quiet pub?

Jody clamped her eyes shut. She'd got herself into this. She was going to have to get herself out. Alone. The way she always had. She'd been stupid thinking she could have a happy ending. 'Get out.'

'But the festival…' Christian's clammy hand touched her shoulder. 'Oh God, Jody. I'm so sorry. It really was an accident. Jordan. Madam Foxy. All of it. I was busy, stressed, tired. I let things get on top of me. Give me a chance to prove I'm worth keeping on. Please.'

She shrugged his hand off. 'We don't need you any more. We'll be fine.' She opened her eyes. '*I'll* be fine.'

Christian's face blanched. 'But it's not all done. There are things still to be sorted. And Jordan will be fine. Don't do this to us.' His hand reached for her again but she dodged it. He tilted his head closer to her. 'And what about the swimming pool? What will you do? How will you pay back your debt to Rabbits Leap if the festival isn't a success?'

Jody cringed. He'd said the words softly, but not soft enough. She didn't have to check the faces of the locals to know they'd heard what he'd said. She could tell they were aware by the rising tide of whispers, building to a low roar, before going deadly quiet again, as if they were afraid to miss out on one second of the drama unfolding before them.

'Christian.' She lowered her voice. 'Don't say another word. Just leave.'

Tony came to stand beside his sister, fingertips resting lightly on her elbow. A show of support? Or was he getting ready to haul her out of there if things became more heated than they already were? 'What's he on about, Jody?'

'It's nothing. He's raving. He doesn't know what he's talking about.'

Christian's stance straightened. Hardness shrouded him. He looked like the man she'd first met. Distant. In control. Used to keeping those around him at arm's length. 'I know exactly what I'm talking about. But I'm not saying another word. I'll leave now. Good luck with the festival.'

Christian went to leave, then stopped in front of Jordan. His lips moved but Jody couldn't make out the words. Whatever he said erased the pain in Jordan's eyes as a smile lit up his face. Christian's hand went to Jordan's hair, spurring Jody into action.

'Don't touch him. You've done enough.'

Christian made no show of hearing her words other than to pull his hand back, then head upstairs. Hopefully to pack his bags and get out of town, Jody thought, ignoring the lurch in her heart that tried to tell her she didn't mean it. Telling her she'd miss Mr Fancy Pants.

'What do you need me to do right now, Jodes?' Tony stood in front of her, protecting her from the prying eyes of the villagers.

'Get me away from this lynch mob,' she muttered, fighting back tears. 'I just want to get Jordan and Tyler home and tucked into bed.'

'He said something about the pool.' Mrs Harper's voice broke the ominous silence.

Jody cringed. It wouldn't take a genius to put two and two together. She was sunk. The game was up.

Mrs Harper broke through the crowd to stand next to Tony. 'And I was checking the festival accounts the other day and no payment had been made to Christian. Which seemed odd. I don't see a man like that working for free. So it leads me to wonder... Who could be paying him? And that leads me to think it's someone with a debt to clear. And why? Because they feel guilty about something... Or, more to the point, *she* feels guilty about something.'

'Jeez, Mrs H, you should've been a private investigator,' Tony joked. 'You could've solved the world's greatest mysteries. Bermuda Triangle. Loch Ness. Jack the Ripper...'

Jody nudged her brother, a quiet 'thank you' for trying to dissolve the tension in the room. But it was going to take more than a joke to fix this. More than an apology too.

'Mum,' Jordan moaned. 'Can we go home? My ankle's really sore.'

The pain in his voice focused Jody. She didn't have time for this. She had to go back to doing what she'd done for the past ten years. Her boys were her priority, not the town, not the pool. She had to take care of them, and that started with getting Jordan home and comfortable.

'Tony. Can you carry Jordan to my car? I'll go grab Tyler. I take it he's upstairs playing video games?'

Tony nodded. 'Meet you outside?'

'I'll only be a minute.' She dared to take a peek at the crowd. Suspicion marred their usually open and honest faces.

'You can't just leave,' Mrs Harper squawked. 'We have things to talk about. Important things.'

Jody turned to face her accuser. 'I can. And I will. But I have to look after my son first.' Not waiting for a reply she hurried upstairs, rushed Tyler out to the car, bundled him in and took off before the mob could follow. She didn't need their pitchforks thrust in her direction. She already felt like one had pierced her heart.

CHAPTER FIFTEEN

Jody paced the sitting room. Five steps. Hit the wall with its framed black and white photo of the boys lying back in the fields, laughter lighting up their faces. Swivelled on her heel. Five more steps. Hit the opposite wall with its painting of the sunrise over the hills of Rabbits Leap, turning the landscape a hazy hue of orange and pink.

Not that she saw the painting. All she saw was a blur. The tears she'd fought back as she put the boys to bed finally given permission to be set free.

How could Christian do this? Keep a secret as big as that from her? Not telling someone who was hiring you that you were responsible for one of the biggest news stories of late was reprehensible, and plain inexcusable. If she'd known he could be so irresponsible, so negligent, she'd never have hired him. Not when she finally had her chance to atone for her misdeeds.

But was he really that negligent? Some rational part of her brain pinged into life, throwing up a bunch of memories to drive the point home. Christian on the phone arranging for the hay-bale pool to be built. Christian hunched over his laptop ensuring every inch of advertising was perfect. Christian holding the boys' hands at the fair after she'd lost them, ensuring they weren't going anywhere.

Stupid rational brain. Sure, he'd gone over and above to ensure the festival would be a success. And she could see he cared for the boys. For their safety. But he'd still hidden something major from her. She couldn't forgive him for that. And he'd outed her act of defiance in front of the whole town. Worse than the whole town, in front of Mrs Harper. Who no doubt was now well and truly putting two and two together to come up with one very guilty Jody McArthur.

Tiredness stopped Jody in her tracks, forced her to sink onto the sofa, to bury her head in her hands. She caught the sound of an engine coming up the drive, a car door slamming, then the inevitable knock at the door. She groaned. Who was here?

Was it Mrs Harper here to have it out with her?

Or Christian come to apologise?

Whoever it was, they weren't welcome. She wiped away her tears, then pushed herself up off the couch. If whoever was at the door asked about her red, puffy eyes, she'd lie and put it down to an allergic reaction. *Yeah, an allergic reaction to a man.*

'Sit, Jodes. It's just me.' Tony's frame filled the sitting-room door.

'You knocked. You don't have to do that. In fact, you never do that.' Jody settled herself back down and patted the spot next to her on the sofa.

Tony sat beside her and shrugged. 'I just thought you might have company... Then I realised it was only your car parked out front so...'

'He wouldn't dare come. Not after what he did. I half expected Mrs Harper to turn up, though. She's like a damn dog with a bone when she gets going.'

'Don't I know it. She was nattering away after you left, so much so I threatened to throw her out and impose a life ban if she didn't shut up.'

'Did she shut up?' Jody pulled her knees up to her chest and hugged them tight.

'The Bullion is where she gets a good chunk of her gossip from. What do you think?'

'Thanks, Tony. And thanks for getting me out of there.'

'It's what big little brothers do for their little big sisters.' He nudged her affectionately, then stilled. 'But we have to talk.'

'About the pool? About whether I was the person who broke it? I was. I did. And I was paying Christian out of my savings to make the festival big enough and successful enough that enough money would be raised to fix it once and for all. Penance.'

'No, not about the pool. Though it's nice to know you're not Little Miss Perfect.'

Jody snorted, then coughed as a glob of snot hit the back of her throat and slipped down her gullet. 'Little

Miss Perfect got pregnant with a man she didn't even know, remember?'

'Yeah, well. You made two perfect young men. Besides, I'm hardly going to judge you for having one night of passion. I'm amazed there aren't any little Tonys running around.'

'So, if it's not about my illegal teenage activities, what did you want to talk about?'

'Not a what. A who.' Tony angled his body towards Jody. His face etched with concern.

Oh hell, no. He wasn't going to defend Christian, was he? Jody bristled. Well, if he'd planned to, he wasn't going to get a chance. 'God, what kind of idiot am I?' She held up her hand. 'No. Actually, don't answer that. I know what kind of idiot I am. I'm the dumb idiot who should have known better. Who should have stuck to her own rules and kept away from the big-city boy. Instead I let his pretty face, fancy clothes and smooth-talking ways seduce me. Well, more fool me, because here I am hiding away in my little cottage, probably about to be frogmarched out of town, my name mud, Jordan hurt, Tyler confused.' Overcome with exhaustion and emotion, the tears began to flow freely. This was all her own fault.

She shouldn't have made love to Christian.

Shouldn't have kissed him.

Should have fired him the day he growled at the kids in the park.

Should never have hired him to manage the festival in the first place.

But mostly, she should never have given herself a glimpse of what a larger, more fulfilling life felt like. The kind of life she'd dreamed of since she was a young girl.

And she should never, ever, have fallen in love with him.

A cry broke free from her aching chest.

In love. She loved him. She'd broken all her own rules, including the biggest one. No love. Not ever.

It never led anywhere good. People who loved you died. Or ignored you. Or left. Breaking your heart. Again and again and again.

Another sob erupted, and another. And another.

How had she allowed herself to fall in love? Allowed herself to be that vulnerable? What had she been thinking, giving her heart to a man who held secrets so close to his chest? Big secrets. Life and death kind of secrets.

Dirty. Lying. Scumbag.

At least she had all the ammunition she needed to make sure she never fell in love again. Ever.

'Jody?'

Jody looked up to see Tony squatting in front of her. At some point he'd wrapped his large, warm hands around hers. An act of silent support.

'I was a fool, Tony. Trusting a man, letting him get close. I should've stuck with my rule. No love. Life would've been simpler.'

'True.' Tony nodded. 'Your life would have been simpler, but you'd have been unhappy.'

'Unhappy? I was never unhappy. I had a great life.'

'But do you still love it? Because there was a whole lot of past tense in that statement.'

Jody bristled, hating that he was right. 'What's that horrid, clichéd saying? 'You don't know what you've got 'til it's gone'? Well, I had a simple, easy life, and then I let Christian get close. Too close. Now...' Jody drifted off, not wanting to admit the truth.

'Now, without him, you actually *will* be unhappy? You didn't give him much of a chance to explain himself back there, Jody. You heard a couple of words and went to town on him. If he means that much to you, perhaps you should talk to him. Find out whatever it was that happened in his past. Get to the bottom of the story. Maybe you could even forgive him?'

'You mean forgive him for lying to me? For failing to tell me he was responsible for nearly causing another person's death? If he'd told me about what happened with Madam Foxy, I'd never have let the boys go with him today. But he didn't. He never said a single word, even after—'

Tony landed a finger on her lips, silencing her. 'Yeah, I don't need to hear the rest of that sentence.' He mimed sticking a finger down his throat and gagging.

Jody snorted and elbowed her brother. 'Oh, ha ha. God, you're a numpty.'

'And you're forgetting you didn't tell Dad you were pregnant until you were nearly two thirds of the way through and couldn't hide your weird skinny arms and legs with a big bulging stomach combo any more. For ages, he thought you'd eaten too many beef pasties.'

'That was different,' Jody protested. 'I was eighteen. And Dad was too hard to talk to... Too wrapped up in his own grief. Hell, when I told him, he grunted and told me to get back to work. He didn't care. God, I think I could count on two hands the times he interacted with the boys.'

'So you're saying you're not hard to talk to? Because just now you shrugged Christian off the way Dad would shrug us off.'

Jody sprang off the sofa and towered over her brother. 'What is this? Are you on his side? Are you saying this is all my fault?'

Tony threw his hands up, warding her off. 'Hell no, not at all. Not even remotely. You're one of the best people I know, and I hate that you're hurting. I hate that he hurt you. I mean, if he ever lays a hand on you again or even looks in your direction, I'll take that fancy car of his and drive it into the smelliest biggest boggiest marsh I can find. I'm just trying to talk you down, Jodes. I'm not used to seeing you so ruffled, undone...'

'"Talk me down"? Oh, I'm down, Tony. I'm calm. Cool as a cucumber. Seeing the world with a clarity

219

I haven't in a long time. There's room for only two blokes in my life. That's it. Jordan and Tyler, and no one else.'

'Not even your poor, long-suffering brother?'

Jody collapsed onto the sofa and hauled her brother up to sit next to her. 'You're not a man. It's like you said, you're my brother. You don't count. It's just, I don't know, I think I'm better off without anyone else in my life. I mean, one week of liking a man and it's already a disaster. I think manless is best for me, and for the boys.'

Even if that means never feeling Christian's touch again? Never inhaling his citrusy scent? Or feeling his lips linger on your skin every time he kisses you, like he doesn't want to let go?

Jody clamped her hands to her cheeks to hide the reddening. Why did Christian have to make her feel so deeply about everything? Why couldn't she just hate him completely like she wanted to? Why must some small, daft part of her still want him?

Love. Stupid love. That was the reason.

Well, she was going to arrow love right in the heart and send it on its way, for good.

'So, do you want me to break into his car and trash it before he leaves town? Which he's doing tomorrow. Not that you want to know that... Or, I could serve him rotten scrambled eggs for breakfast. Although I don't really want to because they'll stink out the kitchen.'

'Numpty,' Jody grimaced. 'Maybe skip the eggs but feel free to trash his car.'

'Ah, you'll probably come up with better forms of revenge. You always did. Hell, you broke an entire pool.' Tony shook his head, his gaze half admiring, half amused. 'So, what will you do when he comes knocking before he goes?'

'Knocking? He won't come knocking. If he knows what's good for him, he'll do as he's said he'll do and get out of town first thing. Besides, if he was idiotic enough to come knocking, I'd kick him so hard in the backside he wouldn't be able to sit for days.'

'But what if he does?' Tony persisted. 'I mean, you two clearly had a thing, so he'll want to talk to you eventually, I'm sure. And, I don't know, if you're so dedicated to moving on with your decidedly manless life, maybe the best thing you can do is listen to him if and when he turns up? Maybe even express how you're feeling in an eloquent manner. What do they call it? Get yourself some closure.'

Jody rolled her eyes and snorted in disgust. 'Geez, look at you, Mister Reasonable. What happened to getting back at him? Has falling in love made you turn soft?'

'Eh, I'm too old for such shenanigans, too responsible. As for these heart-to-heart chats? I only do them once in a very blue moon, so yeah, all I'm saying is, maybe hear him out. Then you can move on, and get happy again. Either way, I've got your back, and I'm always here.'

Jody flung her arm around her brother's shoulders and gave him a squeeze. 'Thanks, Tony. But I'd rather never see him again. I think it would be easier.'

'Up to you, Jodes. Up to you. Well…' Tony slapped his knees, then stood up. 'Time to get a move on. The missus will no doubt be serving half the town beers while listening to tonight's gossip, all while wondering where I am, and in her current condition she needs all the sleep she can get.'

Jody's head snapped round to face her brother. 'What? Did I hear right? Condition? Is Mel pregnant? You're going to be a dad?'

Tony raised his finger to his lips. 'Shhhh, it's early days. She'll stop making my daily scones if she knows I told you.'

Jody lunged at her brother and embraced him in a bear hug. 'Congratulations, Tony. You're going to be an awesome dad. The best.'

'If I'm half as good at parenting as you, I'll be doing fine.' Tony broke the hug and stood up. 'Now go find yourself some happiness, Jodes, you deserve it.'

As she watched her brother leave, Jody lifted her index fingers to the bottoms of her eyes and tried to stem the dampness she could feel welling up.

Damn tears. Back again. But for Tony this time.

Happy tears, she tried to convince herself.

Joyful tears. For her brother. For Mel. For them finding love. For making a baby in their love. Not sad tears. Not tears reminding her that she'd fallen for the wrong guy, and paid the price. Not tears of regret, not tears of anger. Not tears coming straight from her broken heart.

Except they were.

CHAPTER SIXTEEN

When had his flat become so small? So claustrophobic? Christian pushed his laptop aside and fought back the urge to picture Rabbits Leap, with its little lanes, tiny, whitewashed cottages, and poky but perfect shops, all surrounded by a sprawl of land rising and falling until it hit the edges of the horizon, continuing on into spaces unseen.

The horizon at home? A block of flats across the way. Another block opposite. Compacted further by the stark walls of his home. He ran his hand over his jaw, soft lengths of hair grazing his palm. When was the last time he'd shaved? No matter. He wasn't out to impress anyone. Only someone. And she wasn't interested. Not that he'd tried to get in contact. Self-defeat and self-loathing had seen him not send one text. Not make one call. He'd attempted to send an email half a dozen times but only got as far as 'Dear Jody, I'm sorry' before slamming the lid down on his laptop, his stomach a swirling mess of sadness, anger and disgust. He was the failure he'd always suspected he might be. His mother and father would no doubt be saying 'I told you so' if they could see him now.

His computer pinged its incoming email alert. He opened it and scanned the contents. A request for his services. An eightieth birthday party with a 1980s theme, catering for fifty people. So this was his life now. Small jobs. Small life. Well, at least it matched his small heart. His shrunken spirit.

He folded his arms on the desk, burrowed his head into them and cursed himself for the zillionth time. He should have told Jody about the Madam Foxy affair at the beginning. Implored her to trust him. But instead he'd gone on a mission of ego. Determined to prove to himself that one failure wouldn't end his career. Except he now had two failures behind him and word had finally got out in the events industry. His abrupt disappearance and the chef's insistence he'd never received an email from Christian mentioning Madam Foxy's allergy had wound up the rumour mill, which quickly deemed Christian guilty. Of course, as expected, there'd been no messages of condolence, no one reaching out to offer him work. He was tainted goods. His colleagues didn't want to know him, and neither did Jody.

He was a fool to think things could have been different. That he could have been different. For one moment he'd truly thought he could be the embodiment of the opposite of his parents – open, loving, ready to give everything to the person he loved in order to make them happy, ready to sacrifice everything. But as soon as things got tough at the pub, he'd shrugged on the mantle of disassociation that had kept him safe for years. Kept his heart closed and his soul shrouded.

Better to push them away before they pushed you.

Except it was too late. He'd fallen in love. Proverbial head over his proverbial heels. He had tried to push Jody away with words, but he couldn't push away the love.

Another email ping saw him clapping his hands over his ears. He fought the urge to ignore the message but glanced up and the name on the screen refused to be ignored.

Shirley Harper.

He tapped the trackpad and leant in, not wanting to misread a word.

He read it once. Twice. Thrice. Then a fourth time just for good measure.

His tired, heavy heart lightened, just a little. Perhaps he wouldn't have to figure out how to make a living out of catering to the random whims of the general public. Perhaps he would be able to break free from the confines of London life. And maybe, just maybe, he would get a chance to start a real life. A life he could be proud of.

But first, he had to return to Rabbits Leap. No. Wrong. First, he had to shave.

***

226

'Boys. Get a wriggle on, the bus will be here in five minutes,' Jody called over her shoulder as she shoved clothing into the washing machine for what felt like the millionth time that week. For one week now she'd refused to leave the house, the shame of Rabbits Leap knowing what she'd done having become an invisible barricade between her and the world. She'd washed all their clothes, their dirty sheets, their dirty towels, as well as sheets and towels and clothing that didn't need washing. You could eat off the floors. There wasn't a spider's web in a single corner of any room. The garden had never been so weeded. One week and the house was immaculate; one week and she felt empty on the inside. Her initial anger at being lied to had morphed into a nagging disappointment that Christian hadn't even cared enough to apologise, to explain himself. Then, as her phone remained blank, as the driveway remained free of the soft purr of his sleek sports car's engine, she'd come to the conclusion he'd never cared that much about her anyway. She was a distraction, a way of filling in time until the festival was over and he could get back to London. To his exciting, challenging, busy, fulfilling career.

'Boys?' she yelled again as she registered the lack of feet thumping out the door. The absence of a door slam.

Tyler poked his head into the laundry. 'Mum, there's someone here to see you.'

His voice was unusually subdued, almost worried. Who was here? At this time of day? Jody shut the washing machine's door with a bang, prodded at the buttons, and left it whirring and whirling away.

'If it's someone trying to sell something, tell them to come back when we're rich.'

'Mum. It's not someone trying to sell something.' Jordan appeared in front of her, grabbed her hand and pulled her to the front door. 'It's Mrs Harper. And Mrs Hunter. And Mr Brown.'

Mr Brown? Jody wondered if there was time to sprint out the back door and up into the hills. Mr Brown was the big guns. The owner of the local newspaper, stationery store, and more importantly, the current parish council clerk. Had he come to make her pay for the damage she'd done to the pool? Was she about to be escorted to the local policeman? Locked up? Made to pay for her past sins in a small cell?

'Jody?' Mrs Hunter called. 'Come out here, please. We need to talk to you.'

'You've got to go, Mum.' Tyler took her hand. 'They look serious.'

She allowed Tyler to drag her out to the front of the house, Jordan trailing in their wake. She kissed the tops of the boys' heads as usual, keeping it casual so as not to worry them, but she breathed in their earthy cinnamon scent a second longer, deeper, than usual. Just in case she was about to be carted off to jail.

'I'll see you this afternoon.' *I hope.* She waved them off and turned to face her judge and jury. 'So, how much trouble am I in?'

Mr Brown took a step forward and came to stand in front of Jody. His face, usually ready with an easy smile, was sombre. 'Well, it has come to our attention that you might have had something to do with the destruction of the pool.'

Jody pushed away the temptation to get defensive and spout out a teenage-ish 'so what if I did', complete with surly eye-squint and a 'just you try and argue with me' bottom-lipped pout. She settled on crossing her arms over her chest and staring at her feet. 'I guess, at this point, lying about it isn't going to do me any good. So, what do we do about my stupidity from over a decade ago? Will you report it to the police?'

'We could. Some of us talked about it…' Mr Brown's voice trailed off.

Jody lifted her head to see Mrs Harper's face flush. Of course Mrs Harper would have brought up the police. Anything for a bit of extra drama.

'But the thing is…' Mr Brown continued. 'That would leave two good young boys without a mother. A mother who has devoted herself to them since the day they came to be. Don't think we didn't notice that, Jody. The village did. You've been an amazing mother. And the last thing we want to do is leave another child without a parent.'

Jody had a feeling he wasn't just talking about her mother passing away. Mr Brown's wife had fled the village years ago, leaving him to raise his daughter, Tiffany, alone.

'You're being very kind, Mr Brown. I appreciate it. And I do apologise for doing what I did. I was so... confused. Angry. Unhappy. But I should never have taken it out on the pool. On the people of Rabbits Leap.'

'No, you shouldn't have.' Mrs Hunter sidled up beside Mr Brown. 'To be honest, we're hurt you didn't admit to your wrongdoing at the time. We would have worked something out, Jody. You must realise that you belong as much to Rabbits Leap as you do to the McArthur family. Your blood runs deep here, girl. And we knew things weren't easy at home.'

Jody dipped her head, shame heating her cheeks. 'I know. You were all so good to me, and to Tony. I think that's what made it harder to say something to you. I took my anger out on the wrong people. And I'm so sorry I wasn't able to do anything to rectify things until now.'

'Well, that's good, because you're not getting away with this scot-free.' Mrs Hunter's fingers touched the bottom of Jody's chin, lifting it so their eyes met. 'You're not.'

'So what do you want me to do? Pay for it to be fixed myself? I can. I will. But it will have to be in increments. The only other option would be to sell the farm, but...' Jody's stomach flip-flopped at the idea of selling up and moving on. The farm had been her grandparents' home. And in so many ways it had been her home growing up, especially after her mother died. It was the only place she'd felt cared for. Loved.

'We wouldn't ask you to do that, Jody.' Mrs Hunter reached out for Jody's hand and stroked the top of it with her thumb. 'This is McArthur land. It shall stay that way.'

Tears sprang to Jody's eyes at the unexpectedly kind gesture.

'But you're going to have to finish what you started.' Mrs Harper elbowed her way in between Mrs Hunter and Mr Brown. 'That means you have to continue your work with the festival. We're stepping back. You'll have to organise the running of the events. The timing of the bands. Organise what Mr Brown here needs to be saying as the MC. All of it. Starting with finishing off that bloody bunting.' Mrs Harper trudged to her car, opened the boot and pulled out a massive armful of fabric. She staggered under its weight, regained balance and trudged back, dumping it at Jody's feet. 'Marjorie and I started to do it, but it was taking longer to do than we thought. It's good to have it off our hands, right, Marjorie?'

Mrs Hunter gave a brisk nod. 'Right. What Christian was thinking, asking us to make it to save a few bob, I'll never know.'

'And that's it?' Jody had a sneaking suspicion she was getting off too lightly. These were kind people, good people, but they weren't pushovers. Something else must be up.

231

'Well, there is one more thing.'

Don't make me work with Christian. Don't make me work with Christian, she chanted to whichever god of keeping people's hearts stony, their mind sane, was listening.

'If the festival doesn't bring in as much money as is needed to fix the pool, we will expect you to make up the shortfall within the next year so it can be ready for next summer. Are you amenable to those terms?' Mr Brown stuck out his hand.

Jody mentally waved goodbye to her dream trip around Europe once and for all. Unless everyone who bought tickets came and spent a goodly amount, she was going to have to foot the rest of the bill. She shooed away the building disappointment. This was her fault. She'd started it. She had to fix it. She had to finish it. Her hand met Mr Brown's and they shook on it. 'You've got a deal, Mr Brown. And I just want to thank you for dealing with this unfortunate situation so kindly. And I do apologise for what I did. I've carried the guilt with me for so long, in a strange way it's nice to have the truth out there. Although I'm guessing I should hide out here until the day of the festival? People must hate my guts.'

'Actually, Jody…' Mrs Hunter opened her arms for a cuddle. 'They're surprised that's all you did. Despite the unfortunate passing of your mum, and your dad's…' She paused, her eyes looking heavenward as if searching for the right word.

'Emotional unavailability,' Mrs Harper added. 'No point beating around the bush. That's what it was.'

'Well, yes.' Mrs Hunter nodded. 'Despite that, you two are a good couple of kids. I wish you'd rub some of that goodness off on Serena.'

Jody accepted the embrace. 'Ah, Serena's good. She just has her own ways.'

Mrs Hunter's chest heaved as she laughed. 'Don't I know it.' She released Jody and gave her a small smile. 'Now, you go and make this festival the biggest little festival the district has ever seen.' She turned on her heels and made her way back to the car, followed closely by Mr Brown and Mrs Harper.

'The Big Little Festival,' Jody said out loud. The name given to it by Christian.

He'd had such vision for their event. Such passion. And where was he now? Probably at some swanky café having a bit of breakfast, reading the news on his phone, his hair flopping onto his forehead, impatiently shoving it back the way he had time and time again as they'd breakfasted together after their night of lovemaking. Her teasing him mercilessly about the irritations of having a fancy haircut. His laughing as she'd found some nail scissors in her bag and threatened to give him a trim. Being pulled across the small café table into a long and distracting kiss, which only stopped when the scissors clattered to the floor. Abandoned as his kisses had abandoned her lips and sought out her neck.

She shivered despite the heat in the morning sun. Screw Christian. She'd make the little festival big. The biggest ever. She didn't need him to help her. She didn't need him at all. Full stop.

Even if the molten heat pooled low in her stomach said one part of her most definitely did.

***

Serena threw her needle and thread down in disgust. 'I hate bunting. All these stupid triangles. With all the stupid sewing. If I needed yet another reason to dislike *that man*, this would be it.'

Jody nodded her agreement as she tied off the thread and released it with an efficient snip. 'He really stitched us up... Oh well, only another hundred or so to go. Don't abandon me now, Serena. Will more wine help?'

'More wine will always help.' Serena picked up her needle and thread and nodded thanks as Jody sloshed pinot gris into Serena's glass. 'So, the big day's tomorrow. You're all set?'

Jody added more wine to her glass, took a glug and set it down. She suspected there'd be a few more glugs in the offing before the next day. 'I think I've got everything sorted. The parking direction signposts are up. The volunteers are briefed. All of the different activities are manned. The food trucks are rolling in at seven a.m. And once we hang this bunting up we'll be sorted.' She eyed her wine. Maybe she shouldn't have too many more glugs. Tipsiness, ladders and heights probably weren't a good mix.

'So, are you ready to talk about the giant elephant that's been following you around for a couple of weeks now?' Serena asked pointedly.

234

'Elephant? No elephants here. Didn't have any planned for the festival. Wouldn't know where to house one even if I did.' *Screw the lack of glugging.* Jody picked up her glass and took another hearty sip.

'Starts with Chris. Ends in heartbreak?'

'Chrisheartbreak?' Jody pushed her glass away. The wine tasted sour. Or perhaps it was the conversation.

Serena huffed and waved a finger at Jody, setting her bracelets jangling at a rapid clangy rate. 'You need to talk about your feelings, Jody. Bottling them up won't do you any good. Look what happened the last time you didn't express yourself. You took a mallet to the pool, for God's sake. Talk to me.'

'I spoke to Tony.'

Serena groaned and gazed up at the ceiling. 'Give me strength,' she muttered before zeroing in on Jody again. 'Tony's your brother. Which means, for one, he's family, so the way you chat to him is going to be more-holds-barred, because he doesn't really want to hear about your love life. And two, he's a man. So he's not going to really believe how much of a dick a man can be.'

Jody recalled how Tony had talked about forgiving Christian, giving him a chance. Serena had a point. 'So, what should I be telling you since you're, one, not my family. And two, a female.'

'I'd like to think we were close to family, Jody. We've known each other since we could crawl.'

'Well, you've hardly been around for the past decade. It's not like you've been here to care,' Jody retorted. Guilt immediately crashing over her as she saw Serena's face fall. 'Bloody hell, I'm sorry, Serena. My defences go up whenever I talk about Christian. It's the only way I know how to survive this...' Jody searched for the word and came up empty.

'The ache? The emptiness? That feeling there's some really important organ-like part of you missing? Like you've got your lungs, which is great, but you can't really breathe? Like your heart's in there, but it's not beating properly?'

Jody's heart went out to Serena. Considering they were meant to be good friends, best friends, they hadn't really talked about the things that mattered to them. 'We suck at this friendship thing, don't we? You've been back a good few months and we haven't had a heart-to-heart. I don't even know how you're doing. How are you doing, Serena?'

Serena summoned a smile that only emphasised the twinkles of tears. 'I'm surviving. I've got plans. Things I'm hoping to make happen. Soon. But I came home for the right reasons.'

Jody saw the doubt in Serena's eyes. 'You think you've come home for the right reasons.'

'More like I hope I have. Time will tell.' Serena blinked hard. Once, twice, three times. The dampness was gone, but the pain was still there. 'Anyway, we can chat about me and my ridiculousness another day. I'm not going anywhere. Right now, it's you I'm worried about. Have you even heard from him? Has he called and grovelled? And if he has, did you tell him to piss off?'

Jody shook her head. 'But I haven't contacted him either. Then again, I don't think I'm the one who should be apologising. He said he was meant to be on holiday but wanted to keep busy, so that's why he took the job I had on offer. But I don't know. I get the feeling he was running away from that Madam Foxy thing. He used me to hide out. And my kid got hurt in the process. He all but swore his undying love to me, to the boys, to the town. Then when things got tough he upped and left. How could I trust him again? How could I begin to give him a second chance?'

'Second chances are a funny thing. But, I don't know, they happen. They're happening right now.' She held up the bunting. 'I've got needle-pricks in my fingertips to prove it. Have you even looked into the situation? Done a search on the internet? Surely something like that would have stirred up a news story.'

Jody scooped her phone up off the coffee table. 'I haven't. But you can. I don't want to see his face. I'd probably smash my phone if I did.'

Serena took the phone off her. 'Fair enough. If I hear another song or see another picture of... Well, I'm surprised I'm not rocking back and forth in the cowshed. That's probably why I hang out there so much. The only music that's played in there is by dudes who died years ago.' She swiped and tapped. 'Middlemore's his last name, right?'

Jody nodded and focused on the task at hand. Unable to stop her hand trembling, she set the bunting down and scooted over next to Serena. 'Anything?'

'Not interested, hey?' Serena joked.

'Oh sssssshhhhh.' Jody nudged her friend and was rewarded with a giggle.

'Okay, here's some stuff. He was a big-time event manager. But we know that. Oh. Okay, so the word's out that he was responsible for the allergic reaction. There's a statement from him apologising to the concertgoers. Madam Foxy's people have released a statement saying they forgive him. That's gracious of them. Did he have a website?'

'He did. That's how I checked his credentials.'

'Well, he doesn't now. Seems, despite their acceptance of his apology, he's shut up shop. Gone under, no doubt. No less than he deserves,' Serena snorted.

'Well, that's got to be a good thing. No website means no chance of my looking him up. That'll make it easier to push him away.' Jody bit back an 'ow' as the needle stabbed her thumb pad, the pain bringing clarity. 'God, like father, like daughter. I really am a product of my dad. Christian said as much. So did Tony. Always keeping people at a safe distance. Refusing to engage in anything emotional. I don't want to be like my father, Serena. I want to be warm and open, like Mum was. Like I'm pretty sure I used to be once upon a time.'

Serena looked up from the phone, her features softening. 'You're hurting. So badly. I'm sorry.' She wrapped Jody in a cuddle and held her close. 'Perhaps you need to ignore me and my bitter ramblings.

I'm not man's best friend right now. But you know what I think?' she whispered into Jody's hair. 'I think everyone deserves a second chance. You got yours. Perhaps you could extend that courtesy to Christian. Be the person you were meant to be, Jody.'

Jody nodded into her friend's shoulder, pulled back and wiped away the remaining tears. 'Give me my phone.' She pulled up Christian's details, hit the call button and put the phone to her ear.

There were no rings. Just a message in a voice that sounded like Christian's, but less warm, more brusque, instructing her to leave a message after the tone and he'd get back to her as soon as possible.

'Not there?' Serena asked, softly.

'Straight to voicemail. Probably doesn't want to hear from me ever again. Which I deserve. I was harsh, Serena. Mean. Cruel.'

'No, you were an overprotective Mama Bear. Nothing wrong with that. As long as you know when to let your little ones go free.'

'Unlike that mother of yours…'

'I'll be one hundred and she'll still want to tuck me in at night and kiss me on the forehead.' Serena shivered as she eyed the bunting. 'How many more?'

'Same as before. One hundred, give or take.'

'Less talking. More sewing. And more wine.'

Jody picked up the bottle and poured.

'He'll come round, Jody. I saw the way he looked at you. Right from the start he was besotted.'

239

'And if he doesn't?' Jody willed her hands to stop shaking so she could get back to work.

'Then he's missed out on something special. On someone special.'

Jody breathed away fresh tears. 'Well, that would make the two of us.'

CHAPTER SEVENTEEN

Groups of people buzzed along happily, like bees in a field of flowers. Dipping into shops. Gathering around gourmet treats. Enjoying the stickiness of feather-light candyfloss and the soul-warming butteriness of freshly popped popcorn. The weather had put on its own show. Wisps of clouds floated across a brilliant blue sky; the sun beamed down on the village, creating a sea of bare arms and legs that stretched as far as the eye could see.

The festivalgoers were in high spirits, and so were the villagers, based on the series of check-ins Jody had conducted.

'Made five times my day's usual takings so far,' Mr Thompson mentioned to Jody as he restocked his pile of cheeses and meats. 'You're getting free sausages next week. You can have the ones I usually give that chatty Mrs Harper.'

'If I have to make another batch of scones ever in my life I'm going to throw myself head-first into the dough until I breathe my last,' Mel had grumbled good-naturedly.

'No Christian?' Tony had commented as he poured a pint.

'No Christian,' she'd replied, all matter-of-fact. Despite her newly made vow to be more open, more honest, more present in the community that had embraced her from the start, she didn't want to get her hopes up that she'd have the opportunity to practise this newly rediscovered side of herself with Christian. But it didn't stop her heart from hammering against her chest whenever she saw a thick head of impeccably cut, cocoa bean-coloured hair sauntering through the crowd.

'The bunting looks good.' A silky-smooth voice brushed her ear, sending shivers of despair and delight down her spine. Oh great, so she wanted to see him so much she was now hearing things.

'Next year you should definitely mix it up with those coloured light bulbs like we talked about. Bunting by day, a rainbow of colour by night,' commented the voice that shouldn't be there. 'And how much bunting did you do? I can't see the sky for fabric? Did Mrs Harper get the Stitch 'n' Snitch girls to help? They must have sewed their fingers down to stumps.'

She glanced over her left shoulder, following the sound of the voice. She wasn't imagining anything.

Christian.

Finally. The word breathed through her soul.

'Christian.' She nodded as a hurricane of thoughts whipped through her mind. Why was he here? What did he want? Was he here to see her fail? To have the last laugh? Was he here to claim some success so his business could bounce back? Was he here…for her?

'Jody.' Christian's eyes met hers, briefly, before focusing on the bunting again. His hands were shoved deep into the pockets of his khaki chinos. His left foot twisted back and forth on its ball ever so slightly. And his mouth twitched at the corner. He was nervous.

Jody felt the tug of her inner magnet, begging to be allowed to click into him. To be part of him. With him. And she wanted to, but they had a long way to go, a whole lot to talk about, before things could be taken further. Or forgotten altogether.

'So what are you doing here?' she said, taking a tiny step backwards. Creating breathing space. Thinking space.

His gaze settled on her. A little less nervous. A little more open. 'I wanted to see how everything panned out. We put a lot of work into this festival. I guess I needed to see how it was all going to end. Do you know what I mean?'

Jody's heart constricted in her chest, but she held her emotions in check. He wasn't going to see the disappointment anywhere on her face or body. Keep calm. Keep relaxed. There was no point being the new, open Jody with someone who was about to reject you. That openness could be saved for when she was crying into a wine glass at the pub, with Serena, Tony and Mel there to support her. 'Fair enough, so shall I give you a guided tour?'

'Sounds good.'

She waited for Christian to crook his arm so she could hook her arm through as he'd often done before. But he didn't. Jody's heart further tightened. He really was here to see things through. To put an end to his relationship with the town, with her. She straightened up, pushed her shoulders back and adopted a businesslike manner. If that was what he wanted, fine. She'd get over it. Eventually. 'I'm taking it you've already seen the food trucks and bake stall if you've made it this far?'

'I have. I've also been promised sausages by the butcher,' he replied, his lips quirking. 'I guess that little comment you made gave him reason to think Mrs Harper might have opened her mouth.'

'Perhaps, and he does seem in a better mood of late. Maybe he's happy to have people knowing his secrets,' Jody observed.

'I don't blame him. In fact, I can understand. It's easier to breathe when you're not hiding things from people.' Christian stopped short. 'I'm sorry I kept my mistake from you, Jody. I just didn't know how to tell you. Anyway, I'm out of the London game now. I couldn't see it bringing me joy, and without joy, what's the point?'

Jody turned to face Christian. If they were going to say goodbye it might as well be on good terms. 'I'm sorry you've quit the business. But I'm even more sorry for the way I behaved at The Bullion. I shouldn't have gone off on you like that. I should have given you a moment to explain. Jordan and Tyler explained things to me later, much later, when I'd calmed down. But it was too late. You'd gone... And I was too pigheaded to call and apologise.'

'I wish I hadn't gone.' Christian dipped his head. 'I would rather have put up with wave after wave of your wrath than tucked my tail between my legs and bolted back to London.'

'Well, I'm glad you left.' Jody flinched as Christian's eyes registered hurt at her words. She touched his forearm. 'Not because I didn't want to see you. But it gave me time to think. To process. Can we find somewhere a little more private to talk?'

Christian nodded and followed her through the crowds until they came to the school where the ponies were plodding about, grinning children on their backs.

'You kept the ponies? Even after what happened?' Christian followed Jody's example and sank down onto the grass.

'I did. Like I said, the boys told me what happened. Jordan was being a rascal. You stopped him. As you should have. Then he decided he knew better and came off the pony incorrectly. Then you rushed him to the pub to see the doctor. Christian, you did every single thing I would have done. I can hardly blame you for that.'

'Well, I still blame myself for keeping you in the dark right from the start. I should never have let my ego and my fear of failure rule my behaviour. It wasn't right to run and hide. I should have been honest. I can't help but wonder what would have happened if...'

245

Jody held a finger up, silencing Christian. 'No. No "what ifs". We can spend our lives wondering "what if?", but it won't change anything. I know I did for a long time. What if I hadn't fallen pregnant? What if I hadn't had the boys?' She closed her eyes, afraid to see Christian's reaction to her next 'what if?'. 'What if I sent you back to London today and never ever saw you again?'

She paused, waited for Christian to answer, but instead found herself pulled to a standing position. Christian was so close she could smell his scent. Feel the heat radiating off him.

'Jody. There's something you need to see.'

Without waiting for an answer, Jody found herself being tugged back into the crowds, only to be stopped by a stuffed seagull.

'Well, look at you two,' Ms Millie chortled. 'So I was right after all. Of course, I knew that. I see quite the trip in store for you two. A wonderful ride indeed. Now, go do what you have to do…' She tipped her seagull in Christian's direction and carried on down the street in a puff of billowing yellow-and-aquamarine kaftan.

'What's she going on about?' Jody wondered aloud.

'No idea.' But there was a twinkle in Christian's eye that made Jody wonder otherwise. Still, she allowed him to pull her down towards the end of the street where the Ferris wheel held pride of place, turning slowly as happy families, happy friends and happy couples circled lazily around. Except. They weren't. It was empty.

'I grew up being told, and believing, that the only thing that mattered was success, Jody. And that belief took its toll on me. It made me believe it was easier to keep people at a distance than to deal with their inevitable disappointment when they discovered I wasn't perfect. The sad thing was, even with that belief embedded in my head, I continued to work as hard as I did to try and capture the attention of the two people who were never going to care because they were too wrapped up in their own worlds. Too full of their own importance to believe there was any other way than their way.' Christian's face was trained on the Ferris wheel.

Jody laid a hand on Christian's forearm, relief flooding through her when he didn't shrug it off. 'What if you reached out to your parents one more time? Just laid it all out flat and wrinkled on the table. Maybe then you could try and iron out some of those feelings?'

A vein pulsed at Christian's temple, his jaw set then released as his chest rose and fell. 'I actually tried. I had some loose ends to tie up in London. Madam Foxy's management to apologise to. My business to wind down. And in the spirit of a fresh start, I called my parents, told them I wanted a new life, a different one. When they learned it wasn't the life they still, after all these years, wanted for me, they got off the phone as quickly as they could.' A short bark of laughter escaped Christian's lips. 'Anyway, you're right. We can't spend our life wondering about "what ifs".

We can only move forward. Only do our best.' Christian shifted his attention from the Ferris wheel to Jody. 'It's what you did too, wasn't it? Moving forward. Doing your best. You couldn't go to art school, or travel as soon as you would have liked, but you immersed yourself in your passion, in your art, and created some of the most wonderful works I've ever seen. I can't believe you hid that talent away. And when a certain busybody emailed me saying she was concerned about you, saying you'd been hiding yourself away... Well, I couldn't let you do that. A vivacious, beautiful, talented person like you should shine. Not skulk in shadows.'

'Christian, I hardly think sitting at home feeling sorry for myself is akin to skulking in the shadows.' Jody rolled her eyes.

'Well, you hadn't been seen in over a week. And the town was getting worried.'

'Worried? The town were plotting how to make me pay for ruining the swimming pool. I had the two Mrs Hs and the village clerk on my doorstep, forcing me to finish off the festival.'

'Well, it got you out of the house, didn't it?' Christian's gaze fell to meet Jody's. A sparkle in his eyes.

'Oh my God!' She punched him in the arm. 'It was you who organised that?'

'Well, I knew you'd beat yourself up about the swimming pool, and the town's reaction to your teenage actions, until the day you died, unless you managed to make it up to them. So I figured, what better way to do that than to make you accountable for your mistakes.'

'How do you know me so well, when we've only known each other such a short time? How did you see that I was becoming the person I never wanted to be? How did you, of all people, get me to open up? God, what would I have become, *who* would I have become, if it wasn't for you.' Jody held her breath as tears attempted to rise. She forced a smile and reminded herself that Christian wasn't here for her. He was here to tie up loose ends before moving on to the next step in his life.

'I think the question is, how did you make me into the man I didn't know I wanted to be?' he replied. He took her chin between his thumb and forefinger and caressed it. 'Maybe we're just good for each other.'

'Like two magnets whose poles just click,' Jody murmured under her breath.

'Just like that.' Christian cupped her face, the sweetest of smiles lifting the edges of his lips. 'Now, Jody, I need you to do something for me. Look up.' He tipped her head towards the Ferris wheel.

A lump formed in Jody's throat. Mrs Harper was waving madly at her. Sitting next to her was one of Jody's paintings. Below her Mrs Hunter was grinning, and gripping another work.

'You did this?' She looked to Christian, then set her sights once again on the Ferris wheel as painting after painting circled, held by those who had come to be nearest and dearest to her, now that she'd allowed them into her heart.

'Your talent needs to be seen, Jody. It shouldn't have to wait until the boys have left home. Neither should your happiness. I hope you don't mind, but I took the liberty of pricing them and a fair few have already sold. I think you'll have enough to take the boys on that trip you've always dreamed of.'

'No.' Jody crossed her arms. 'Not until I pay for the pool. That's my first priority. This town's been so good to me, I need to make things right.'

'Well, I don't think that's going to be a problem...' Christian nodded at the fundraising thermometer that had been set up on the stage. Mr Brown was busy painting the white void red, up, up, up...

'Oh my gosh, they did it!' Jody jumped up and down, clapping her hands. 'The town did it. You did it.' She went to throw her arms around Christian, but stopped herself. 'Congratulations.' She stuck out her hand, meaning for him to shake it.

He grabbed her hand and pulled her to him, wrapping his arms around her waist. A swarm of local kids, dressed in the rabbit costumes she'd designed, scuttled up the street and surrounded them, whooping and hollering as they were being chased by the local band, playing as terribly as ever. But there was a voice among the tuneless playing. Rich, soulful...

'Is that who I think it is?' Jody strained to see above the crowds who'd gathered, their hands clapping in time to the beat of the music, their cheers reaching fever pitch.

Christian grinned. 'Madam Foxy – officially the most un-diva-like-diva in the world.'

'But how? Who? You?' Jody gazed up into the eyes of the man she wanted to spend the rest of her life with.

Christian's grin widened. 'I asked her management if I could make a personal apology after what I'd done. They reluctantly agreed. And so we talked, and somehow this great big story of this tiny little village came out. And then I might have mentioned meeting the one woman who's made me want to turn my life upside down, who's made me want to be a better man. There may have been a brief moment of very unmanly sobbing. And then she offered to help out. A show of no hard feelings. Why do you think the place is crawling with television cameras?'

'I thought that was because of the interest we'd had from the regional station about the attempt we were making to create the world's largest slip and slide.'

'How did that work out?'

'Turns out we can design rabbit costumes, inspire grumpy butchers to get behind a community initiative and organise a festival in three weeks, but we can't count.' Jody grimaced, then laughed. 'We were about five feet short. But that's okay. We'll try again next year. We'll need something to top having Madam Foxy drive out the rabbits with her voice. I can't believe you did this for us...'

'I did it for you, Jody. You're an amazing woman. And this is an amazing town. I count myself lucky to have been part of it, even if only for a few weeks.'

'So what happens next?' Jody's stomach went into free-fall. This was it. This was goodbye.

'What happens next is I pack my bags.'

'And go.' Jody fixed a smile on her face. If Christian had made up his mind, she wasn't going to make him feel bad about his decision. He'd had enough to feel bad about in his life.

'Yes.' Christian nodded. 'And go.'

'Well, it was good while it lasted.' She attempted a light-hearted laugh, but it came out high-pitched and brittle.

'What?' Christian's head jerked back. 'What do you mean?'

'You're heading back to London. Your job is done. Why? What did you mean?'

'I meant I'd pack my bags in London and move here. I've already looked at a place I could rent, and I've had a chat to Mr Brown about helping with the Christmas parade, and Mrs Hunter very kindly said I could be her lackey when it was time to organise the Farmer of the Year Awards. My website's being updated to reflect my availability for creating bespoke small-town events throughout Devon, with Rabbits Leap as my base. After today's success I don't think I'll be hunting for work.'

'You're going to start a business here? And rent a place?' Was he saying what she thought he was saying?

'Well, I have to have somewhere to live and a job to do if I'm going to move to Rabbits Leap, don't I? I've also been in touch with some art galleries and there's one in Tiverton that's very excited to display your works. The owner said, and I quote, that you are the "discovery of the year". You just give me the nod and I'll arrange everything.'

Jody's heart thumped as fast and hard as the clapping of the crowd's hands. Not that she could register their excitement at being metres away from the world's most popular pop star, due to the rushing of blood in her ears. 'You know, you were right about me being like my father. Even when I tried not to be, I was. But I've been working on being less like him and more like what I'd like me to be.'

Christian inched Jody closer. 'And just how would you like to be?'

Jody swallowed. It was now or never. 'I'd like to be someone who isn't afraid to tell you how I feel. The thing is, Christian, I can't imagine you not being in my life. I want to make you endless cups of tea, and I want to spend the rest of my life teasing you about your fancy hair. Although I don't know how you'll keep that cut up if you're living here in Rabbits Leap. The hairdresser does short back and sides and that's about it.' Jody took a deep breath. It was time to dive in, sink or swim. 'What I'm saying is that I'm madly, ridiculously and totally in love with you. And I want nothing more than for you to be part of our family…if you'll have us?'

Christian's head dipped towards Jody. His lips lingered above hers. Then touched. Soft. Sweet.

She breathed him in. Then pulled him down, kissed him harder, her fingers raking his hair, her body arching against his as he brought her even closer, oblivious of the fever-pitched cheering as the fundraiser thermometer overflowed.

They broke the kiss, but remained fused together.

'Is that a yes?' Jody asked, breathlessly.

'Will I take you, your family and this town with its big heart to be mine?' Christian grinned. 'It's a yes.'

Before she could kiss him again, Christian whipped her off her feet and spun her round and round, until the festival was a blur.

'Hey, no fair!' Tyler ran up to them and tugged on Christian's shirt. 'Me too!'

'Then me!' Jordan jumped up and down.

Christian set Jody on the ground and held her steady. 'Who needs the tipsy turn of a carousel? The mad sugar rush of a candyfloss binge? Or the heady heights of a Ferris wheel?' Christian kissed Jody, then brought the boys in for a group hug. 'I have a feeling I'm in for the ride of my life.'

**Turn over for an exclusive extract from the first
in the Rabbits Leap series by Kellie Hailes:**
The Cosy Coffee Shop of Promises

CHAPTER ONE

'Wine. Now. And don't get mouthy with me.'

Mel watched Tony's sea-blue eyes light up as his lips parted slightly...

'What's got your knick—'

'I'm serious,' she cut in, before he had a chance to be the second person to grind her gears that day. 'I'm in no mood for your cheek. And I can tell by that twitchy jaw of yours that you're contemplating still trying to give me some.' Mel took off her navy peacoat and shuddered as wintry air wrapped its way around her thin form. She promptly buttoned up again and tugged her scarf tighter around her neck. 'All I want from you is for you to do your job, pour me a glass of pinot gris and leave me to drink it, alone, and in peace. And why is it so cold in here? It's freezing out. It shouldn't be freezing in.' She shook her head. 'No matter. I don't care. The wine will warm me up.'

'Bu—'

'No. No buts. No whys. No questions.' She pointed to the glass-doored fridge. 'Just get the bottle, get a glass, and pour.' Mel gave Tony her best glare, hoping to get past his notoriously thick skin.

She watched the muscles in his jaw continue to work, as if debating whether to ignore her order to be left in peace or do that clichéd 'had a bad day, tell me about it' barman patter. Sensibility must have won, because he turned and bent over to grab a bottle of pinot gris from the chiller, giving her a fantastic view of his toned and rounded rear. A view she'd usually take a moment to appreciate, but not right now, not after the unexpected, and not in a good way, phone call she'd just received from her mother.

Tony sloshed the wine into a tired-looking, age-speckled glass, pushed it in her direction, then punched at the card machine. 'Here you go,' he said, proffering the handset.

Mel squinted at the numbers on the screen. 'Tony, um, that's not right. You've overcharged me.'

'No, that's the price.' Tony nodded, but kept his eyes firmly on the bar. 'Since the beginning of this week.'

'Really? You can't tell me a bottle of wine rose in price by almost double in the space of seven days?'

'You're right, it hasn't.' He glanced up. 'But the hole in my muffler is yelling at me to put the prices up. And I haven't in years, so...'

'Oh. Okay. Sorry.' Mel handed over her bank card, embarrassed to have questioned the price rise. She'd heard the village gossip. Tony's business wasn't doing so well. Apparently hadn't been for years, but had got worse since his dad passed away the year before. Not that she knew much about that. She'd been new to town, and didn't want to get a reputation as a gossip, so had only heard the odd conversation here and there over the coffee cups in her café, nothing more.

'So, are you going to just stare into that glass of wine or are you going to drink it? Because I don't have a funnel to pour it back into the bottle. Although reselling it would make my mechanic happier faster. And if you buy two glasses I might even be able to afford to put the heating on.'

Mel shot Tony a grateful smile. Despite his infamous reputation as a ladies' man, he was also known about the small farming town of Rabbits Leap as being something of a gentleman and had quite the knack of making you feel at ease, which, considering her current heightened state of irritation, was quite a feat.

'You're still not taking a sip, or a slug. And, well, it sounds like you need a slug.'

Mel narrowed her eyes at Tony, hoping to scare him into shutting up with a stern look. 'What did I say about getting mouthy? And teasing for that matter?'

'I'm not teasing. You look pale. Paler than usual, and you know you're pretty pale, so you're almost translucent right now. Even the bright streaks of pink in your hair are looking a little less hot.'

'You pay attention to my hair colour?' Mel's hand unconsciously went to her hair and tucked a stray lock behind her ears. Tony looked at her hair? Since when? She'd always assumed he'd seen her as nothing more than a regular customer, a friendly acquaintance, not someone to take notice of. Sure, they got along well enough, would chat for a moment or two if they passed each other on the street, or if it was quiet in the pub, but that was the extent of their relationship.

'Well, you're about the most exciting thing to happen in this place for the last ten years...'

'Me? Exciting?' A tingle of pleasure stirred within her.

Tony winked and turned that tingle into a zing. Since her last boyfriend, the local vet, had taken off to care for animals overseas, Mel hadn't had any action, let alone a compliment, from a man. And apparently, if that unexpected zing frenzy that had zipped through her body was anything to go by, she'd been craving it.

'Yeah, exciting.' Tony's glance lingered on her face, as if drinking her in. 'And pretty, too.'

She rolled her eyes, trying to ignore the way her body reacted to the words of approval. She picked up her glass and took the suggested slug. She was being stupid. Tony wasn't calling *her* exciting, just her hair. And the only reason he was calling her pretty was because that's what he did; he called women pretty, he charmed them, he took them to bed, and that was that. And she'd had enough of her love life – heck, her life in general – ending with 'that was that' to be interested in someone who'd pretty much created the phrase.

'Feel better?' His eyes, usually dancing with humour, were crinkled at the corners with concern.

'Not really.'

'Have another slug.'

As she lifted the glass she glanced around the bar, taking in the bar leaners with their tired, ring-stained, laminated tops and obsolete ashtrays in their centres. The tall stools next to them looked rickety from decades of propping up farmers, the pool table needed a resurface, and as for the dartboard, it was covered in so many tiny pin holes it was amazing a dart could stay wedged in it. The village chatter was right, Tony was doing it tough...

Her eyes fell on a machine sitting at the far end of the bar. All shiny and silvery and gleaming with newness. That shouldn't be there.

Her blood heated up, and not in an 'oh swoon, a man just complimented me' kind of way.

'What is that?' Mel seethed through gritted teeth.

She couldn't believe what she was seeing. What was he thinking? Did he have it in for her, too? Was it 'Let's Piss Off Mel Day'? She'd moved to Rabbits Leap just over a year ago to try and create a sense of security for herself. A place she could settle down in, call home, maybe even meet a nice, normal guy she could fall in love with. And in one day what little security she'd carefully built was in danger of being blown apart. First her mother calling to tell her she was coming to town and bringing her special brand of crazy with her, and now this?

260

'What's what?' The crinkles of concern further deepened.

'That.' She pointed to the cause of her ire.

'The coffee machine?'

'Yeah, the coffee machine. The coffee machine that should not be in your bar, because I have a coffee machine. In my café. The only café in the village. You remember that? The one place a person can get a good cup of coffee? The place that just happens to be my livelihood, and you want to screw with it?'

Tony took a step back as if he'd been hit with a barrage of arrows. *Good*. His eyebrows gathered in a frown. But he didn't look sorry. Why didn't he look sorry? And why had he straightened up and stopped looking stricken?

'It's just business, Mel.'

'And it's just a small village, Tony.'

She looked at her wine and considered throwing the contents of it over him, then remembered how much it had cost. Taking the glass she brought it to her mouth and tipped it back, swallowing the lot in one long gulp.

She set the glass back on the bar, gently, so he wouldn't see how shaken she was. 'There's only enough room in this village for one coffee machine.' She mentally slapped herself as the words came out with a wobble, not as the threat she'd intended.

'And what does that mean?' Tony folded his arms and leant in towards her, his eyebrow raised.

Mel gulped. He wanted her to throw down the gauntlet? Fine then. 'It means you can try to make coffee. You can spend hours trying to get it right, make thousands of cups, whatever. But your coffee will never be as good as mine and all you'll have is a big hunk of expensive metal sitting unloved at the end of your bar.'

'Sounds like you're challenging me to a coffee-off.'

How could Tony be so cavalier? So unfazed by the truth? He'd spent a ton of money on something he'd only end up regretting.

Mel took a deep breath, picked up her wallet and walked to the door. She spun round to face her adversary.

'There's no challenge here. All you're good for is pulling a pint or three. Coffee? That's for the adults. You leave coffee to me.'

She leant into the old pub door, pushed it with all her might and lurched over the threshold into the watery, late-winter sun and shivered. Could today get any worse?

Had he done the wrong thing? Was buying that ridiculous monstrosity and installing it in the pub a stupid idea? He'd spent the last decent chunk of money he had to get it. What if it didn't fly? What would happen next? He couldn't keep the place open on the smell of a beer-soaked carpet, but he couldn't fail either. It was all he had left to remind him of his family. The Bullion had been his dad's baby. The one thing that had kept his dad sane after his mother had passed away. More than that, it was where what few solid memories he had of his mother were. Her smiling at him as he sat at the kitchen table munching on a biscuit while she cooked in the pub's kitchen. The violet scent of her perfume as she'd pulled his four-year-old self into a cuddle after he'd fallen from a bar stool while on an ambitious mountaineering expedition.

Then there was the promise he'd made to his father, the final words they'd shared as his father breathed his last. His vow to preserve The Bullion's history, to keep her alive. Dread tugged at his heart. What if he couldn't keep that promise?

God, why couldn't his father have been more open, more honest with him about their financial situation? Why couldn't he have put away his pride for one second and seen a bank manager, cap in hand, asked for a… Tony shoved the idea away. No. That wasn't an option. Not then. Not now. The McArthurs don't ask for help. That was his dad's number one rule. A rule his father had also drilled into him. No, he wasn't going cap in hand to a bank manager. He didn't even own a cap, anyway. He just had to come up with some new ideas to breathe life into the old girl. The coffee machine had been one of them, and he'd spent the last of his personal savings buying it.

But what if Mel was right? What if he couldn't make a good coffee? Heck, what if she stole into the pub in the middle of the night and tampered with it so he couldn't?

Tony shook his head. The potential for poverty was turning him paranoid. Besides, the coffee machine was a great idea. Lorry drivers were always stopping in looking for a late-night cup, and who knew? Maybe the locals would like a cup of herbal tea or something before heading home after a big night.

Buy herbal tea. He added the item to his mental grocery list, along with bread, bananas and milk. Maybe he'd see if there was any of that new-age herbal tea stuff that made you sleep. Normally he'd do what his dad had always done and have a cup of hot milk with a dash of malt to send him off. But lately it hadn't done the trick and he'd spent more hours tossing and turning than he had actually sleeping, his mind ticking over with mounting bills, mounting problems and not a hell of a lot of solutions. Heck, he was so bone-tired he wasn't even all that interested in girls. Maybe that was the problem? Maybe he needed to tire himself out…

'Hey, baby brother!'

'Might be. But I'm still taller than you.' Tony grinned at his sister and two nephews as they piled into the pub. 'How you doing, you little scallywags?'

'Scallywags?!'

Tony laughed as the boys feigned insult and horror in perfect unison.

'You heard me. Now come and give your old uncle a hug.'

The boys flew at him, nearly knocking him over as they hurled themselves into his outstretched arms.

He drew them in and held them, breathing in the heady mix of mud and cinnamon scent that he was pretty sure they'd been born with.

'Have we cuddled you long enough? Can we have a lemonade now?' Tyler peered up at him with hopeful eyes.

'And a bag of crisps?' asked Jordan, his voice filled with anticipation, and just a hint of cheek.

'Each?' They pleaded in perfect unison.

Two peas in a pod those boys were. And the loves of Jody's life. Since the day she'd found out she'd fallen pregnant to a man she'd met during a shift at the pub, a random, a one-nighter, she'd sworn off all men until the boys were old enough to fend for themselves.

Tony watched as the boys grabbed a bag of crisps each and poured two glasses of lemonade and wondered at what point Jody would decide they were old enough, because at nine they looked pretty well sorted, and he was pretty sure he spotted flashes of loneliness in her eyes when she saw couples holding hands over the bar's leaners.

'So what's with the shiny new toy?' Jody jerked her head down towards the end of the bar.

'It's what's going to save this place.'

Jody snorted and took a sip of Tyler's lemonade, ignoring his wail of displeasure. 'It's going to take a whole lot more than coffee to save this dump.'

Tony bristled. Just because this place wasn't the love of her life it didn't mean it wasn't the love of his, and just as she wouldn't hear a bad word said about her boys, he didn't like a bad word said...

'And don't get all grumpy on me, Tony McArthur. I know you love this joint, but it needs more than one person running it. You need to...'

'If you say settle down, I'll turn the soda dispenser on you.'

'Oooh, soda water, colour me scared.'

'Not soda, dear sister. Raspberry fizzy. Sweet, sticky and staining.'

Jody stuck her tongue out. 'But you should, you know, settle down. It'll do you good having a partner in crime.'

'You're one to talk.'

'I'm well settled down and I've got two partners in crime, right, boys?'

Tony laughed again as the boys rolled their eyes, then took off upstairs to his quarters where his old gaming console lay gathering dust.

'Besides, you're only going to piss off the café girl with that machine in here. You're treading on her turf, and frankly it's not a particularly gentlemanly thing to do.'

Heat washed over Tony's face. Even though he had a reputation for liking the ladies he always tried to treat them well. But that was pleasure, and this was business. Not just business, it was life and death. Actually, it was livelihood or death. And he intended to keep on kicking for as long as possible. Without the bar he was nothing. No one.

'Well, I can see by the flaming shame on your face that she's seen it.'

'Yep,' he sighed. The more he looked at the hunk of metal the worse he felt about what he'd done. There was an unspoken rule among the business people of Rabbits Leap that they didn't poach customers. It was akin to stealing. Yet he'd done just that in a bid to save The Bullion. What was worse, he'd done it to a member of the community he actually respected and always had time for.

'Tony, you've got to apologise, and then take the machine back. Do something. It's a small town and the last thing you need is to be bad-mouthed or to lose customers. Find a way to make it work.'

***

Ting-a-ling.

Mel looked up from arranging a fresh batch of scones on a rose-printed vintage cake-stand to see who'd walked in, her customer-ready smile fading as she saw her tall, broad-shouldered, blond, wavy-haired nemesis.

'Get out.' Her words were cool and calm, the opposite of the fire burning in her veins, in her heart. No one was taking away her café, her chance at a stable life, especially not a pretty boy who was used to getting what he wanted with a smile and a wink.

'Is that any way to treat a customer?'

'You're not a customer. You never have been. I've not seen you step foot in here since I opened up – not once.' Mel pointed to the door. 'So get out.'

'Well, maybe it's time I decided to change that. And besides…'

She watched Tony take in the quiet café. Empty, bar her two regulars, Mr Muir and Mrs Wellbelove, who were enjoying their cups of tea and crosswords in separate silence.

'…it looks like you need the business.'

Mel rankled at the words as they hit home. She'd hoped setting up in Rabbits Leap would be a good, solid investment, that it would give her security. But that 'security' was looking as tenuous as her bank balance. The locals weren't joking when they said it was 'the town that tourism forgot'. In summer the odd tourist ambled through, lost, on their way to Torquay. But, on seeing there was nothing more than farms and hills, they quickly ambled out again. As for winter? You could've lain down all day in the middle of the street without threat of being run over. And this winter had been worse, what with farmers shutting up shop due to milk prices falling even further.

'Really? I need the business?' She raised an eyebrow, hoping the small act of defiance would annoy him as much as he'd annoyed her. 'I'm not the one putting prices up. Unlike someone else standing before me…'

Tony threw his hands up in the air as if warding the words off.

Good, she'd got to him.

'Look, Mel, I'm not here to fight.'

'Then what are you here for?'

'Coffee. A flat white. And a scone. They look good.'

'They are good.'

'Then I'll take one.' Tony rubbed his chin. 'Actually, make that two.'

Mel faked ringing up the purchase on the vintage cash register she'd found after scouring auction sites for weeks and weeks. 'That'll be on the house.'

'That's a bit cheap, isn't it?' Tony's lips lifted in a half-smile.

'It's on me. A man desperate enough to install a coffee machine in a pub clearly needs a bit of charity.' Yes, Tony was trying to take business away from her, but really, how much of a threat would he be to her business anyway? It wasn't like he could actually make a decent cup of coffee.

'So, are you going to stand there staring at me like I'm God's gift or are you going to give me my free scones?'

Mel blushed.

'Sorry, I wasn't staring. Just…'

'Imagining me kissing you. Yeah, yeah, I know. Don't worry, you're not the first woman.'

'I wasn't.' Mel sputtered, horrified. 'I wouldn't.'

'I know. I'm teasing. Relax.'

The word had the opposite effect. Mel's body coiled up, ready to attack at the next thing he said that irritated her.

Why was he having this effect on her? Usually nothing ruffled her feathers, or her multicoloured hair. She'd weathered so much change in her life that something as small as someone making an attempt to kill off her coffee business should be laughable. But as she looked into his handsome and openly amused face she wanted to take up her tongs, grab his earlobe in its metal claws, give it a good twist, then drag him to the door and shove him out of it. Instead she picked up the tongs, fished two scones out onto a plate, added a pat of butter and passed the plate to him.

'Can you just…sit. I'll bring your coffee to you.'

With a wink and a grin Tony did exactly as she asked, leaving her to make his coffee in peace. The familiar ritual of grinding the beans, tamping them down, smelling the rich aroma of the coffee as it dripped into a cup while she heated the milk relaxed her, so much more than a man telling her to relax ever would. Maybe the problem wasn't that he was trying to ruin her business; maybe it was that he was trying to take away the most stability she'd had in years.

After her café in Leeds had shown the first signs of bottoming out, Mel had sold while the going was better than worse and decided to search out a new spot to move to. She'd had two rules in mind. One, the place had to have little to no competition. Two, after moving around for so many years, she finally wanted to find a place she would come to call home. So she'd packed up her life, headed south, and stumbled across Rabbits Leap after getting lost and motoring about inland Devon with a perilously low tank of petrol.

The moment she'd seen the pretty village filled with blooming flower boxes, kids meandering down the main street licking ice creams without parents helicoptering about them, and a store smack bang in the middle with a 'for rent' sign stuck to the door, a little part of her heart had burst into song. The plan had been to settle down, set up shop and make enough to save and survive. But, as she watched Tony flick through a fashion magazine, she could see her plans to make Rabbits Leap her forever home go the way of coffee dregs – down the gurgler.

She picked up the coffee and walked it over to Tony's table where he was stuffing his face.

'Your coffee.'

'Thish shcone is amazhing.' Tony swallowed and brushed crumbs from his lips and chin.

Full lips, strong angular chin, Mel noted, before mentally swatting herself. She wasn't meant to be perving at the enemy. 'Well, it's my grandma's secret recipe, so it should be.'

'Can I have the recipe?'

'What part of secret do you not understand?' She set the cup down with a clank.

'Sit.' Tony pushed out the chair opposite him with his foot.

'I've things to do.'

'Sit.'

Mel huffed, then did as she was told.

'So how are things?' Tony picked up the cup and took a sip, giving a small grunt of appreciation.

271

'That's how good yours are going to have to be.' Mel folded her arms across her chest and tipped her head to the side. A small show of arrogance, but for all the things she wasn't great at, she knew she could cook and make a damn good cup of coffee.

'It's good to know the benchmark.' Tony's voice was strong but she was sure a hint of panic flashed through those blue sparklers of his. 'Anyway, this isn't about me. How are you? I haven't seen you in the pub with that vet of yours for a while now.'

Mel narrowed her eyes in suspicion. 'Have you been staking me out? Figuring all the ways you can try and horn in on my bit of business?'

'Rabbits Leap makes a habit of knowing Rabbits Leap. We keep an eye on our own. We take care of our own…' A tightening of those lush lips. A moment of regret? No matter. He'd given her ammunition.

'You take care of your own by taking over parts of their businesses? My, how civically minded you are.'

'I know you're annoyed about the machine, Mel, but you don't have to be sarcastic about it. Can't we deal with the situation like adults?'

Mel's grip around herself tightened as her irritation soared. 'I can be whatever I want in my café. And I can say whatever I want, however I want, especially when dealing with a coffee thief. What's next? You'll be calling my beans supplier? Good luck with that. They know what loyalty means.'

Tony's lips thinned out more. Good. She was getting to him. Giving him something to think about.

'As for the vet? Not that it's any of your business but we're over. He decided small-town veterinary work wasn't for him and headed over to Africa to work with wildebeest or something like that.'

'Thought he would.'

'Really?' Mel's chin lifted in surprise. She'd never thought Tony was the kind of guy who delved below the surface of anything. With that easy smile and light laugh, he seemed... Well, about as shallow as one of the puddles that amassed on the main street after a spring shower.

'Yeah, he had that look about him, the "this place will do for now" look. I've seen it before. I knew it was only a matter of time before he left.' Tony picked up his coffee and took a sip. 'God, this really is good. Is everything you do this good?'

Mel's ears prickled hot. Was she imagining it or was that a double entendre? She met his blue eyes and saw not a hint of sparkle or tease. Nope, no double entendre; he wasn't trying to pick her up.

'I guess that means I was "this girl will do for now",' she said out loud, more to herself than to Tony.

'Then he was a fool. A man would be lucky to have a pink-haired barista and amazing cook loving him, cooking for him and making his morning coffee.'

'That sounds more like a slave-master relationship than a real, true-love one...'

273

'I'm sure the man would repay you in other ways.'

This time the sparkle was definitely in his eyes.

'I'd make sure he did.' The words came out before she could stop them, along with a wink. *Traitor.* She dipped her head to hide the flush creeping up over her cheeks. How dare her body flirt so easily with the enemy, even though, with his kind words, he was acting more like a friend. Or someone who might be angling for something more than that. Not that she'd ever sleep with the enemy. Uh-uh. No way.

Taking a long, slow, cooling breath she looked up into Tony's eyes. Something flashed through them. Something quick, hot, fierce. A heck of a lot like desire. Had he been thinking about her...with him? Mel shook the thought clear. Nope, that'd never happen. They were chalk and cheese. Besides, there was no way she was playing around with the local lothario. He didn't tick any of her boxes. Well, not all of them. Hot. Yes. Fun. Yes. But he couldn't commit. She'd heard the village gossip. He was a one-man band. No woman lasted more than a night. Anyway, he was hardly boyfriend material. He only loved himself, and he was obviously careless with money, which meant careless with security, and that was the one thing Mel was always careful about.

'So why did you come here, Tony?'

'I need to apologise and then we need to have a conversation.'

Mel sat up straighter in her chair. An apology? She hadn't seen that coming. 'So, apologise.'

'I'm sorry I bought the coffee machine. Actually, I'm not. But I'm sorry you had to find out about it like that.'

'Not much of an apologiser, are you?'

He at least had the good grace to look slightly ashamed.

'Well, I'm hoping we can come to an arrangement about it.'

'Really? How about I arrange for it to be removed and you go back to bartending?'

'How about you teach me how to use it…and maybe even teach me how to cook?'

Mel couldn't believe what she was hearing. Was Tony mentally deficient?

'Cook? What are you on?'

'That smell, what is it?'

Mel sniffed the air and remembered she had lamb shanks slow-cooking in a tomato balsamic jus in the back kitchen.

'That's my dinner.'

'It smells amazing.'

'Don't try and distract me.' She waved her hand in impatience. 'Why would I teach you my whole trade? Coffee and baking? I'd be out of business within weeks.'

'No, I don't want to know how to bake. I'm talking about learning to cook real food, like whatever it is you've got going back there.' Tony's eyes sparkled with excitement.

Mel could almost see the ideas forming in his head. His whole demeanour was changing in front of her eyes, energy fair sparking off his disturbingly muscular body.

'You've seen the food we do at The Bullion. It's all deep-fried and artery-clogging. I need to get with the times, update the menu, make it appealing, *maybe* even get entertainment in on special nights, see if I can't pull in a few more punters. Turn the place into a tourist attraction, or something. Which would be good for your business, too...'

Tony leaned forward and placed his hand over hers.

Pull away.

But she couldn't. Tony's fingers tightened around the outer edges of her fist, warm, strong, capable. Hands that knew how to work. Weren't afraid of getting dirty...

Did he work out, she mused, as her eyes travelled up the length of his legs and settled on his stomach. Was there a six-pack hiding beneath that grey T-shirt? Strongly defined, hard thighs underneath those denims? Biceps made for picking a woman up and pinning her to a wall...

Get it together, girl! She squeezed her eyes shut, hoping not seeing Tony would stop those unneeded images forming in her head. It didn't work. Was this the effect he had on women? Is that why he was known for having a string of them? Was he truly irresistible?

'So are you going to help me? Or are you too busy meditating over there?'

Mel tugged her hand out from under his and rubbed her face wearily. It had been a long day. Between her mother's announcement sending her stomach into free-fall and the revelation that the man sitting opposite her had decided to pit himself against her in the business stakes, she was ready to go to bed. Alone.

'What's in it for me?' Mel opened her eyes to see Tony giving her a charming smile.

'The pleasure of my company?'

'I'm not seeing anything pleasurable about your company.' The lie came quick and easy.

'Well, maybe it's time you did.' Tony's teasing tone was back. 'Look, how about this for a deal. You help me create a dinner menu, maybe show me how to make a decent coffee…'

Mel's eyebrows shot up, her hackles rising.

'…and I promise to not serve the java until your café closes at…'

'Three.'

'Three it is.'

'I still don't feel like it's a good enough deal for me to give you this much help…'

'Any wine you drink at the pub will be free for the duration of your help?'

The teasing tone was tinged with desperation. Tony had alluded to things not going great, things needing fixing, but maybe he was in deeper than he was willing to let on? And maybe – an idea flitted about her mind – he could help her with her latest drama, the drama that was about to blow into town any day now...

'Okay. I'm insane for doing this, I'll probably regret it with every fibre of my being, but okay. I'll help you... But you've got to do one more thing for me.'

'Anything. Just name it.'

Mel screwed up her courage and forced the words out before she could talk herself out of them. 'I need you to be my fiancé.'

ACKNOWLEDGEMENTS

To all those who read, blogged, tweeted and showed support for *The Cosy Coffee Shop of Promises*, thank you, thank you, thank you. Your love for Rabbits Leap means the world to me, and I really can't thank you enough. Here's a few more though... Thank you, thank you, thank you!

To my husband. Thanks for your continued support, and for putting up with the clickety clack of the keyboard going off in your ear during early mornings and into the depths of night.

Natalie Gillespie. What would I do without you? Every single time I ask 'how do you say this in England' you put me right and correct my Kiwi-isms. Bless your cotton socks.

To my wonderful editor, Victoria Oundjian. Your suggestions, your advice, your thoughts are invaluable. You're a treasure, and working with you is truly a pleasure.

ONE PLACE. MANY STORIES

Bold, innovative and
empowering publishing.

FOLLOW US ON:

@HQStories